Upper Room Diaries

Upper Room Diaries

Dean & Tammie Carter

Upper Room Diaries

Copyright 2016 by Dean Carter. All rights reserved.

This novel is a work of fiction. Names, descriptions, entities, and incidents included in the story are products of the author's imagination. Any resemblance to actual persons, events, and entities are entirely coincidental.

Published by Dean and Tammie Carter

5162 Oliver Road

Flowery Branch, Georgia 30542

678-865-6658 | carter.deanw@gmail.com

Book design copyright 2018 Dean and Tammie Carter

Cover Design by Tammie L. Carter

Interior Design by Dean W. Carter

Published in the United States of America

ISBN: 978-0-9833619-1-6

Fiction / Religious

Dedication

This work is dedicated to my Lord, Jesus Christ as a written work of worship. Just as Able offered up a lamb of innocent blood, without spot or blemish, I bring to you, that which you have has given me, wrapped within the veiled oracle of Lydia, my offering of praise and worship. Given with innocence of heart, a seed to grandchildren I may never see.

To my most precious gift, ever given to me by my Lord, my wife of 37 years and counting. Tammie L. Carter. The one in whom, when I am not listening, the Holy Ghost always has her ear. God chose Eve, the woman, to bring forth life. And without TLC, this work would have never come to fruition.

To our four outstanding children;

Kevin Leviticus

God, first gave us the law.

Johnny Sunrise

God's son rose from the dead, with healing in his wings.

Shabach Gabriel

Shabach; Praise, shout that drowns out whinners and complainers.

That Gabriel would shout praises before the last trump.

Tehillah Tamiym

Tehillah; Praise, hymn that brings Ramah, Revelation, Illumination.

Tamiym; Up right, whole, truth, integrity, nothing missing, nothing.

broken.

I dedicate this work to all, of our, 'children's children'. Godly children are the Lord's inheritance. May God bless you with many.

I pray this work may be useful in your hands. Amen.

Table of Content

Table of Content

Table of Content

Chapter One

Heavenly Herald

"What does an Angel look like? Did God really, just send one to me? I know what I saw and I know what he said, but is my husband going to believe me?"

Her mind raced as she darted down the steep, leaf covered hill back toward the main tent. "I have to tell him what the Angel said but how?" Margaret Ann was out of breath and she could hear her heart pounding as she made it to the creek. She paused, ever so slightly looking for patches of ice, just before hopping onto the first rock. Carefully zigzagging from stone to stone crossing the knee deep, fast water creek, then leaping for dry ground.

Her right foot plunged into the mountain stream. Quick as lighting, out she came but it was too late, she could feel the ice, cold winter water squeezing through her stocking and her foot was beginning to cry for help. Half stepping over to a fallen tree, she took a seat and started unlacing her boot.

It was the winter of 1919 in the Cohutta Wilderness at the southern tip of the Appalachian Mountains, just inside the Georgia State line. Margaret Ann knew this land well since, from her youth, her family always came here during the winter to harvest meat and nuts. It had been a rough year for a lot of folk, President Wilson had a very bad stroke just a couple months before and we were still at war with Germany.

This was the first winter hunt her husband had attended since returning from serving in the Army. Manoah Elbertson was born in these mountains and was fondly known by all as the 'Hillbilly Prophet.' Not only could he quote almost any scripture story, chapter and verse, but important people would come from hundreds of miles away to ask him about his "Tapestry of Times". He seemed to be able to write the headlines for any paper, two or more years in advance.

Margaret Ann and Manoah had been married for five years and they couldn't be happier, except for one small thing. No child. Manoah didn't let it show but Margaret Ann knew in her heart that it meant the world to him.

She was lacing back up her boot, which was still wet and cold, as she thought about what her mother said of Manoah before they were married. "Little Ann" she'd say, "All men are driven by something. Some by money, some by power, some by hate, some by the need for attention and others by women. That boy Manoah is a teacher and is driven by love. Give him lots of children. A teacher without students is like a bird without a sky."

She started making her way down the trail along the winding creek bank. She had to cross the creek six more times before reaching camp but safely managed not to fall in. She saw Manoah standing with a few others by the fire. They watched her as she came up and placed her wet foot as close to the fire as she could without burning her boot.

"Been fishing?" her brother asked, as everyone kinda chuckled. She looked up at Manoah. He knew something wasn't right. "What happened? Why are you out of breath?" he asked. Her younger cousin joined in, "did ya get run by a bear?"

It seemed to just come out without any forethought, "I

saw an Angel". Everything suddenly got deathly quiet. Her mother and the other women that were in the tent must have been listening as they just emerged and surrounded the open fire pit. The men folk just tighten in a little closer.

She thought for a moment, her eyes never leaving Manoah's face, she could hear the fire popping, the sound of seriousness in the rustling leaves under the feet of everyone gathering around. Her senses were alive to the tiniest of things, the feeling of heat on one side of her boot, her hair slightly moving on her neck from the breeze that follows the creek downstream, the smell of oak on the fire and even the fact that Manoah had not blinked. His eyes laid hard like a man who loves people but had seen war.

The silence seemed eternal, Manoah never moved a muscle, he just stared. He was a man that seemed to weight his words before he spoke. The silence broke as he softly said, "That's a real serious thing, would you explain?"

Margaret Ann looked around and then back to Manoah, "Early this morning, I went to the top of Cohutta Mountain to watch the sun rise from above the clouds. As I sat there, I was thinking how the scripture says, 'eye hath not seen, nor ear hath heard, nor hath entered in to the heart of man, that which God hath prepared for them that love him.'. I was thinking how God must have enjoyed walking the earth with Adam and Eve. The sun had just come up over top of the clouds that covered the valleys like white bed sheets. The trees that were on top of mountains seemed to rest on top of the clouds like islands appear on an ocean. God seemed bigger than the world and I just began to pray. I asked him when I would have a child." Manoah's eyes opened a little wider. She continued, "The clouds seemed to rise up following the sun and it wasn't long before the clouds surrounded me. It wasn't as cold inside the cloud. I stood up and told God thank you and I suddenly felt as if I wasn't alone but not in a scared way.

A man walked straight up in front of me and said, 'No longer question in your heart Margaret Ann, if you will have a child. For no longer will you be childless. The LORD has chosen to hide a treasure within your seed, to be released in the fourth generation. By this season next year, you shall bring forth a woman child, her name shall be called, Brigit Fayth for she will be a bridge for the LORD's faith to cross. Then, when her season is due, she will bear a woman child whose name shall be called, Brigit Grace for she will be the bridge of grace that faith may pass. When her season is due, she will also bare a woman child whose name will be Deannah Brigit for she will be the Teaching Bridge. Then will the treasure be revealed unto you in her child. The teacher will bring forth a woman child whose name will be called Lydia Fayth.

In the fourth generation the LORD shall restore the land to his people, for the sins of the Darwinites will have met its full measure. Now, go unto your husband and have him answer my oracle. Why was Paul forbidden by the Holy Ghost to preach the word in Asia?'

The man turned and walked straight back the way he came. In just a few minutes, the clouds lifted and the sun lit up everything. When I looked to see where the man had gone, it was a cliff. The rocky cliff off the east side of the mountain facing the sunrise. He had walked through the clouds on to the cliff and then back through the clouds, off the cliff. He came from the rising sun and returned back to the rising sun."

She finished speaking and instantly her legs began to give way. Manoah and her brother grabbed her and sat her down. She said, "I feel like I just ran a race. I'm shaking but I'm not cold." Her mother and the other women huddled around her.

The men looked at Manoah, "What does it mean? Anything like this ever happen in the scriptures?" her brother asked. Margaret Ann's father was just crossing the creek, "you boys want to drag one in? It's only a hundred yards down creek."

He had been listening from across the creek and out of respect, didn't want to interrupt while she had been speaking. Three of the younger boys took off with grins and giggles.

"What you think Franklin? Did you hear it all?" Manoah asked. Franklin was a big man. Strong, tall and full of joy for life and family. "Yes sir. Heard it all. Don't doubt it a bit. Always told ya'll God was in these mountains. The way I see it, I be having me a granddaughter up here next year. Only thing I'd be thinking about is answering that question he asked you, but that's because I'm fifty, four and you're twenty, nine."

Manoah looked back to the brother, "To answer your questions, kinda yes and kinda. Judges thirteen is where my folks got my name. It was Samson's father and likewise, Samson's coming was foretold to the mother by an angel of the LORD and she too was childless. But, the four generations thing, I'll have to study on that. And I don't remember ever hearing about the Holy Ghost not letting Paul preach. That doesn't even sound right."

Franklin spoke up, "No ya don't have to look for the fourth generations prophesy, that's Abraham and the sins of the

Amorites in the fifteenth chapter of Genesis. But, but, but, wow! If you were to follow that pattern, that was when God brought the children out of Egypt with ten plagues and let the plagues come on unbelievers but not on his people. Son, if that is the case, we all gotta whole lot of studying up and praying up to do.

What are we supposed to teach these children? I don't know about the Holy Ghost not letting Paul preach but I know the name Lydia is in the Macedonian call and her name means Trust and the name, Macedonia means Mixture. It was where the Romans sent different nationalities of people to prevent any one group from starting an uprising. Kinda like a multicultural country".

Manoah extended his hand down to help Margaret Ann up from the ground. She placed her arms around him but it was he pulling her closer. She softly asked him, "are we going to have a baby?"

The crowd was still quiet, not knowing what to expect. Manoah smiled as he glanced around the listening faces, "Don't call me the prophet. You just predicted four generations of girls. I think us men folk are outnumbered.". The tense ice finally broke as everyone fell into laughter and the heavy winter air was filled with the voices of a happy clan.

Margaret Ann reached for her mother and as they joined hands, mother and daughter made their way into the big tent, with a bunch of smiling women following close behind.

The Evening Hunt

Later that day, the men went about doing what they were there for, hunting. Franklin, Manoah and the men had discussed nothing else but the bible since the morning. As they parted on the way to their stands, Franklin told Manoah, "I'll be praying for you son." Manoah smiled awkwardly and with an edginess he said, "I don't think He's listening, He's talking to my wife." Franklin smiled back and continued on his way.

Manoah found his way to the top of the ridge and snuggled in between some fallen trees. The trees were so large it was like having a private room. He had found this ridge to be a good afternoon hunt, years back when he came along with Franklin's family but the fallen trees reminded him of what he called, 'The Law of Change'.

The most consistent thing man is faced with from birth is change. He had told many people over his life, "from the day you come out of the womb, you will have to do things, learn things and experience things you have never done before. Get used to it. Change is constant." He thought how most people hate change, even do everything in their power to stop it. He also thought how right now, he wasn't sure how to handle it himself.

He kicked off the top of an old dead stump and sat down. He leaned his rifle against a tree, reach into his pack and pulled out his Bible. Opening it to Acts chapter sixteen, which he knew was the Macedonian Call and bowed his head to pray, "Lord, my life is not my own. What you would have me do, is what I desire to do. I was not expecting this gift and therefore I

17

am not ready. Make me ready, open my eyes that I may know thy will for this child."

He raised his head and fighting back tears of sincerity, he looked down at his Bible and his eyes fell upon verse six, ' Now when they had gone throughout Phrygia and the region of Galatia, and were forbidden of the Holy Ghost to preach the word in Asia. There it was in black and white. He must have read that verse a hundred times during his life but it had never registered. Why would God not allow Paul to preach?

He thought back to his youth, when his pastor and church had laid hands on him, asking God to enlarge his gift. They called him the 'boy prophet' and the preacher quoted Numbers 12:8 saying the LORD would speak in 'dark speeches' which meant, puzzles or riddles.

What did the Angel call it to Margaret Ann, 'Answer my oracle'? He knew an oracle was a story that circled back to the beginning and had no end. A cycle or pattern without end. The answer had to be hidden in the pattern of this story. Hidden in plain sight for thousands of years but why now? Manoah had to fight back the feeling, "why me?" because he knew this had something to do with women and how God used them. And how He was going to uses them now. He knew it was about a girl child and depositing God's will in the earth. There had to be something in this story.

He knew Paul couldn't get the job done for some reason and that Asia Minor was the chess board God was going to show him why. He went back to reading with an open mind and heart to find out what his wife and soon to be daughter were supposed to do.

It was only a few hours and darkness had fallen. He heard the shuffling leaves across the valley trail. "Franklin?" Manoah called. "Yeah son, you alright?" he replied. Manoah scurried down the moonlit slope, "If I was any better, I'd have to fly! I feel like I am sixteen again."

Franklin had not seen this type joy since church when he was a boy, his dad called it, 'the old folks are getting lit again. They just keep going to the alter and God keeps lighting them up.'. Franklin's dad had been a moon shiner until the LORD showed up one night.

"Boy, slow down or you will be flying". All the way to the camp, the sounds of the waterfalls, the moon light peeking through the two-hundred-foot tree top canopy, the sharp tingle of a winter night dancing on your open skin, Manoah kicking sticks like playing kick the can, Franklin couldn't help but be absorbed by the energy that radiated from Manoah in every direction. By the time they made it to the last crossing, the light from the camp fire shown across the creek.

Margaret Ann, her mother Elisabeth and the others saw the two men coming, laughing, staggering and stumbling. Margaret Ann asked, "Are they hurt?" Elisabeth responded, "I'm trying to figure out who's holding who up". By that time, Franklin and Manoah landed next to the fire, Franklin pointing at Manoah, both laughing too hard to speak. Franklin tried to regain himself and between laughs he said, "I was holding him down. Didn't want to have to climb a tree to get him."

By now almost everybody was infected, giggles, laughter and an occasional snort. One of the boys asked, "Are they drunk?" And Franklin got out "Lit!", then lost it again. Everyone knew the two patriarchs had never drank and would never, but today had been everything but normal and the laughter just kept bubbling out.

It took a while before things began to calm down. The women set the tables with the evening meal and everyone took their place. Franklin stood up to pray which standing to pray was not normal for him, so it drew everyone's attention even more.

Everyone joined hands and he began, "Father, it is beyond me to know how to thank you for all your goodness. Just to be here in the majesty of the works of your hand is above all joy that can be described. To be surrounded by love, and family, and peace, on every side, is too large a blessing for my heart to hold. It forces my soul to speak your praise to all that can hear. And to receive your word today that America is still in your plan for the redemption of man and our son and daughter are to bring forth that seed, has our hearts dancing outside our body. I am a hollow man. My heart is with you, my mind is with you and my body is here. Bless our gathering and our meal in your Name. Amen.

Campfire Message

It was time for the evening message. Everyone gathered around the fire as Manoah and Margaret Ann came out of their tent together. Franklin and Elisabeth sat back in their chairs and the boys brought up armfuls of firewood anticipating a long meeting.

After opening in prayer, Manoah titled the message, "Things I Know and Things I Don't". "First, let me go over with you, what I have found out about the question posed to me from Margaret Ann's visitor. He said, 'Answer my Oracle'. An oracle is like a circular puzzle where you are given a starting point and you journey around the story until it illuminates a truth and by doing so, returns you to where you started and reveals why you had to begin there.

In Acts chapter sixteen and verse six, the Holy Ghost forbid Paul to preach the word in Asia. Naturally, this draws us to the question, 'why?'. Next in the order of the story, we have Paul being called to Macedonia in a vision. After arriving Paul went on the Sabbath day down to where the women met to worship. I found this odd, for it was not Paul's custom to go unto women. I cannot find anywhere else in scripture where he did.

But the first woman to receive the word was Lydia, whose name means 'Trust'. Which is also the name to be given to our fourth-generation child. As I read the entire story, several things struck me about this Lydia. She was a business woman, a seller of purple and she owned her home and was direct and forceful. She said to Paul and his companions, 'If you have found me faithful', which means trustworthy, and then she constrained them the scriptures says, which means forced them to change their minds.

All this being said and, with a complete following of Paul's journeys from that moment on. I would like to read to you a scripture from the book of Revelation chapter one, verses three and four, blessed is he that readeth, and they that hear the words of this prophecy, and keep those things which are written therein: for the time is at hand. John to the seven churches which are in Asia: Grace be unto you, and peace, from him which is, and which was, and which is to come;

Please notice the phrase, 'seven churches which are in Asia'. But God did not allow Paul to preach in Asia. How then do we have seven churches and ninety percent of the New Testament? This brings us full circle back to Lydia.

Now, this is what I know, the answer to the Oracle is Lydia. But if we stop there, we miss being illuminated. When studying scriptures, names have meaning. If I were to tell you there was a rattle snake in the tent, you would instantly understand the character and nature of that name. As it was during the bible times, names of people and places had an understandable meaning to all. The name Judas means 'praise' and the name Iscariot means 'worldliness'. This is a spirit that we still see today in people that choose worldliness over right and wrong.

In the scriptures the word for name was 'Shame', which means 'character and nature'. Lydia means 'Trust', this would be her character and nature, so it should be said that Paul was sent to Macedonia, in Asia, to find the spirit of Trust. Trust was the key God used to open-up all of Asia. And that key was bestowed unto a woman, not Paul. I believe it is safe to conclude, 'no Trust, no Churches in Asia'. A business woman who can be trusted, a strong-willed woman who can be trusted, and a teacher that can be trusted. It appears that God deposits this type spirit of trust in women.

Secondly, I was not asked about the importance of the fourth generation but it stands to reason that I should examine scriptures applying to this. God says, 'He is the same yesterday, today and forever and I am the Lord, I change not'. The scriptures show us patterns and in Proverbs chapter twenty-nine, verse eighteen He tells us, 'where there is no vision, the people perish'. The word vision means oracle and perish means to slowly pass away.

In Numbers twelve, verse six, it is said that when God speaks to a prophet, He will do so in visions. That word vision means, patterns, templates and oracles.

So, we examine Genesis chapter fifteen where God tells Abram that his seed will be slaves for four generations and He will bring them out with a mighty hand. Here we find that in four generations there will be a great divide among the people. We find great plagues and many children dying. We see a great army attacking God's people. We see animals dying, insects multiplying and water polluted. We see heavy hearts, worried minds and the Angel of Death. We also see four generations between the Old Testament and the New.

In the Old Covenant God redeemed the body through Law, in the New Covenant God redeemed the soul through Faith. Could it be that in four generations that God shall redeem the Spirit through Trust?

This brings me to what I don't know. I don't know how to teach these children. That is why, Margaret Ann and I have decided to ask God to show us how to accomplish this. We are returning to the mountain to pray at sunrise, for God to grant us this wisdom.

One of the younger boys said, "That way you can see for yourself if it was an Angel or not". This drew a quick response from Manoah, "I already know! Margaret Ann said so. You could use a dose of trust yourself." Franklin added, "Boy, I think we need to get your believer fixed".

23

At that, a few chuckles bounced around the fire as the sounds of the creek hastened bedtime prayers.

Morning Prayer

The temperature had dropped a good bit during the night. By the sound of the wind at the top of the mountain, it was goings to be an iceberg sunrise. The valley was cold but at least it blocked off the wind. By the time we reached the top, Manoah had faced me and placed his back to the wind, in order to guard me from it. We sheltered ourselves against a large oak and sat down to pray.

Manoah picked up a small acorn, holding it up for me to see, he asked, "know what's hidden in this"? I shook my head no. He said, "The exact same size tree that is protecting us is hidden inside this acorn, but it has to die to be released." He then pulled out his hunting knife, dug a hole in the ground and buried the acorn.

We bowed our heads to pray, Manoah began, "Lord, we have returned here to learn how to raise the children you spoke of to my wife yesterday. In the story of Samson's mother, you returned the following day to speak to both wife and husband. In faith, I am following that pattern and pray for thy grace. Amen".

I pointed to the clouds in the valley, "They're brighter today than yesterday. I wander if they will make it up this high with the wind blowing so hard?" The sky was clear and crisp, like a crystal clear looking glass. The sun broke the crest of Blood Mountain and filled the sky with the brightness of

Heaven.

Manoah whispered, "The sunrise is a diamond that man cannot buy, but if you watch it, you may wear it all day". I was taken by the beauty of the sunrise. It was like the great halls of Heaven's castle. The clouds blanketed the floor, the pristine sky blue painted it's ceiling and the brilliant brightness of truth and love filled the untouchable temple of God.

Manoah pointed to the clouds below the cliff. They were beginning to whirl around as the wind that was on us seem to join in the choir of sights and sounds. It took only a minute or two before the whirling clouds were all around us. One second a thick cloud was on our right and it blew by us, hiding the trees on the left. It was like the Angels had come down to dance on earth.

I noticed a thick bright cloud coming up the cliff that was moving straight toward us. I looked at Manoah and he was looking at it too. In just a second, there he stood, face to face with Manoah. He had a grey beard and weather worn skin. Long curly grey hair and he had a bow in his left hand, a quiver on his back and five arrows. His clothing was dark, robe like and looked as if he had been in a battle for a long time. They stood looking at each other for a moment and Manoah spoke, "Sir, are you to be worshipped?"

His response was soft but firm, "No. I am not. I am the Lord's messenger".

Again, Manoah began, "Sir, the answer to the Oracle is Lydia, the spirit of trust. How are we to raise these children you spoke of and what is to be taught?"

The Angel reached and took out four arrows and placed

them in Manoah's hands, holding them there with his, "This is the Lord's gift unto you. You hold four generations in your hands. You are the watchman of the South Gate. Our Lord spoke of the 'signs of the times', and your tapestry of time allows you to see their days. You shall teach them the exterior journey and how to tell time on the wheel, Margaret Ann shall teach them their interior journey and the secrets of women. Lydia Fayth shall have many challenges in her making, starting with unbelief and she must chose to return to South Gate and die to self to receive her final gift and to fulfill her call. She must, of her own free will, return. Her will cannot be broken, because she must lead many back through her wilderness. If she returns here at the end of the first cycle of time, then you both shall be granted three days to teach her. This can only be done if she can open the South Gate and let you return.

I couldn't hold back any longer, "Sir, what is this, secrets of women?".

He pulled out his final arrow, placed it in his bow and shot into the thick clouds above. We heard the sound, of it hitting something solid, then a flash of lightening and a deafening sound of thunder that seem to shake the ground where we stood. Down came an ancient style chest slowly landing between us. "This is Lydia Fayth's final gift. It comes to you from Lydia of Thyatira, the seller of purple. She spent all her earthly treasures to purchase the diaries of the women that were in the upper room at the day of Pentecost. The secrets of women who the Lord taught for forty days after He came from the tomb. Their diaries and the diary of the seller of purple are within this chest. You shall learn them and you shall teach them to all the children and upon Lydia's return to South Gate, you shall teach her, that she may then release them upon the earth. For this is the Lord's will, concerning the coming age and the four generations. You are to pen a letter of invitation to her today, date it, seal it and place it with your magistrates, to be delivered unto her in the twenty ninth year of life. Hers is the beginning of dark times but light is given to freedoms land for the blood of patriot saints cry out.".

He turned and walked back into the clouds, the clouds lifted and the Lord's Archer was gone. I turned and looked at Manoah. He was looking at me, holding four arrows with tears streaming down his face. We both fell to our knees and touched the chest. I began to cry uncontrollably, "My God, My God! The Diaries!"

Chapter Two

The Office

What am I not doing? What do I need to do? Who is taking responsibility for whom? Who am I taking responsibility for? Who has the power? Who is the rescuer? Who is the victim? How do I know? Have I agreed to more than I want to do? Am I doing more than half the work? Am I owning my power? Am I using it to set my own boundaries? What boundaries do I need to set? Am I using my power to take care of myself? What am I feeling about this situation? What would I like to feel? What action do I need to take to make sure that I deal with this in the best possible way so that it has the best possible outcome?

Lydia was sitting in her office going over her job performance update. It was not good, in fact since she had moved from being the best population projections analysis at the Census Bureau to manager of a department at the Congressional Budget Office, her department has developed into an administrative road block. She was second guessing everything her key staff was doing and she was working longer, overseeing more of their work and still not solving the delays.

So, she pulled out her self-evaluation outline that had always helped her in past struggles. Trying to assess her next moves in the game, before her two o'clock meeting with the boss, who was not happy at all. She was sure that her job may be on the line as she glanced at the computer screen saver that bounced the date and time around like a pinball in a rubber box.

December 17, 2010 - 12:17 PM. She hit the mouse and pulled up a spreadsheet to lay out a matrix for the game theory. Her mind was active but not attached.

She was still going over the blow up she had with her husband the night before. She glanced out the window at the snow-covered streets of Washington, DC. She thought about how much she loved her new office in the Hart Building and how hard she had worked at the census bureau for many years and played the game just right to land her knew managerial position in the congressional budget office. Her marriage to a DC journalist was the best move she had ever made. It opened the doors to all the right people and right places. It didn't take a year before she landed this position. But he didn't get the memo that he was just a taxi driver in the game and now he is talking about having children.

She thought, "Has he lost his mind?" Many times, over the past year she had tried to figure him out on the game board. Often, he would laugh and tell her she couldn't calculate love. When he would get really, mad, he would always remind her of what her stepfather said to him before the marriage, "Robert, She's an Actuary. She treats everything and everybody as an equation. Her complete world view is nothing but laws and formulae, no realities, no drama, no good, no evil, no yesterday or tomorrow, just the mathematical now."

The intercom buzzer went off and startled her. "Mrs. Jackson, there is a certified letter here for you.", the secretary announced. "Bring it in." Lydia smiled as she thought about her choice in receptionist. Joanna came through the door smiling, "Are you ready for the office party? Today is the last day at work until next year and it's Friday!" she touted.

Lydia faked a smile and said, "Can't wait. What's your plans for the holidays?" Joanna handed her the letter and pulled out tickets, "Cruisin! We're headed south baby, south. Caribbean Cruise!" "Wow. Got a spare ticket?" Lydia stood and walked around the desk. "Robert and I are at it again because he wants to have children. I think I'd like to get lost for a week or two." Joanna's face changed to serious, "Oh Mrs. Jackson, a Caribbean cruise would be just what you and he would need.", she said smile a seductive grin.

"Oh NO!", Lydia responded, "We're not having any children. My mother would freak!" Joanna, with a puzzled look, "Your mother? What does she have to do with it?" Lydia smiled, "Mom is a professional woman and she raise a professional girl. She may be a little soft in her social life but she's on her 'A' game when it comes to business. Children are not a part of the plan."

Joanna just shrugged and Lydia gave her a gentle hug in somewhat of a professional manner, seeming to remind Joanna that she was out of place in her office. As Joanna was leaving she turned and said, "Mrs. Jackson, there is something strange about that letter. The delivery guy said it was dated December 17, 1919. He wasn't sure if it had been lost or what, but it was addressed to, ' Lydia Fayth Jackson, Hart Building'."

As the door closed, Lydia returned to her desk and picked up the letter. The sender was Margaret Ann Elbertson, South Gate Plantation, Georgia, 12-17-1919, making a mental note that today was also 12-17-2010. She glanced at the stamp, it was a three cent, 1919 Victory stamp with a deep red violet on it and it had been postage stamped and forwarded from a law office in Ellijay, Georgia. Carefully opening it so she wouldn't damage the stamp, there was a two, page letter inside that she unfolded and began to read.

The Letter

My Dear Precious Lydia,

I am your great, great grandmother and you are my most precious angel, listen to my story.

There was a lady who collected the most beautiful art works of Angels. Everywhere she went, she would go to the finest shops, in search for a "One of a Kind" Angel.

One day, as she passed by a small shop, she glanced into the window and saw one of the greatest Angel figurines she had ever seen. She went into the shop and asked to see the piece. As the Angel was handed to her, much to her surprise, the Angel spoke! You don't understand, the Angel said. I haven't always been an Angel. There was a time that I was nothing more than dirty red clay. My Maker took me and pulled on me and pushed on me and turned my life upside down several times. I finally cried out, what do you want from me? But He just said, "Nothing yet".

Then He placed me on a spinning wheel. Suddenly everything in my world was spinning out of my control. I couldn't tell which way to go, so I cried out, Please Stop! Everything is going to fast! What do you want from me? Again, He just said, "Nothing yet".

Just as things began to slow down, I was placed in the oven. I never knew life could get so hot. I wandered why my Maker was against me so. Did He want me to burn out? I could see through the window of the oven. Everyone on the outside appeared to be doing fine. I pounded on the glass and cried out, Oh God, get me out of this mess. What do you want from me? Again, He just said, "Nothing yet".

Finally, the door was opened and He put me in a place to cool off. I thought to myself, the worst must be over. I had no more than thought it, when He returned and started brushing me with all sorts of colored liquids. The fumes were so strong that I thought I was going to choke. He was so close to me, I could hardly breath. He stepped away for a moment and I thought how the liquid felt like glue. I was stuck. I couldn't move and could hardly breath. Just as I started to complain, He put me back into the oven. This time it seemed to be twice as hot as before. I begged and I pleaded, what do you want from me? Again, He just said, "Nothing Yet".

I knew my life was over. There was no one to turn to, no one could save me from this. There was no hope, I knew I wasn't going to make it. Suddenly, the door was opened and He took me out, set me on solid ground and walked away. My mind raced with fear of what could be next. I stayed there for years. My mind could only imagine what would be next. I thought, maybe this was a test. Maybe I didn't live up to what He wanted. Maybe He has left me because He has rejected me. Maybe, for whatever reason, I just wasn't good enough. Days and days went by and finally I knew, this was as far in life that I was ever going to go. I had reached my final resting place, "Rejection".

Then one day, there He was. I was excited, but just as quickly, I remembered my fears. As He came near to me, I trembled. He stopped just in front of me and held up a mirror and said, "Behold what I have done to you". With tears streaming down my face, I couldn't believe what I was seeing!

Could this be me? It was a beautiful work of a Master. How could this be? I am just dirty red clay. Then He said, "From this day forward, you shall speak for Me."

I looked at Him and asked, "What do you want from me?" This time He said, "I want you to remember that I will never hurt you. I know it hurt when I pushed and pulled and turned you, upside down, but if I had left you alone, your life would have had no shape. I know when your life was spinning out of control that you didn't think I was there, but had I stopped the spinning, you would not have had the strength to stand alone. I know when you went through the fire, that you thought I didn't care, but if I had turned down the heat then you would have become too fragile and would never be hard enough to last. I know when I brushed you with liquids, that you almost choked, but if I hadn't, your life would not show forth the colors of My touch.

And if I had not put you back through the heat, you would not survive the test of time because your first hardness was outward and true strength comes from tempering the inside. That is why the fire was twice as hot. But now, you are exactly what I had in mind when I started.

Now it is time for you to learn the Secrets of Women and release this light into a dark world. Lydia, the Lord gave me a gift that is to be given you in your twenty ninth year. I have kept it safe and it will be the most precious gift you have or ever will receive. It is the diaries of the women in the 'Upper Room' on the day of Pentecost. If you will come to South Gate before Christmas, Manoah and I have been given permission, by the Lord, to give it to you personally and teach you for three days. You have only five years before great challenges come to America and a few years after that, before the great darkness begins. You must deliver this light to those chosen to carry it to the people.

Lydia, you are my Angel and I know the hardships you have endured, but you must come of your own free will and learn how to open Heaven's South Gate so we may come to you. When you arrive, instructions will be waiting, give our love to your mothers.

Love, Margaret Ann Elbertson

Stunned, Lydia sat back in her chair staring at the matrix on the computer screen. Mind racing through her youth, she recalled how she was made go to church. How she would hear the older people down talk the preacher and others in the church. She made up her mind by her first year in college that she didn't want any part of that type friendship and it hasn't hurt her by not having it.

She picked up the phone and dialed her mother. It rang five times and she was about to hang up because she knew the answering machine would pick up on ring number six and she hated those machines with a passion.

Suddenly her mother answered. "Hello", the sound of heavy breathing in the back-round. "Hello mom, It's me. I only have a minute. Are you going to be home this evening? You'll never guess who I got a letter from today.", Lydia waited.

The phone was silent, so much so that she asked, "Mom, are you okay?" Deannah responded, still out of breath, "Damn it. No, damn it. You just landed this job. No, no, no, not now. You got the letter from grandma Margaret, didn't you?" Lydia almost dropped the phone, "You knew about the letter? Why didn't you tell me before now?" Deannah asked, "What did it say?"

Lydia glanced at her screen saver that took over the computer again, 1:23 PM, "Mom, I got a meeting at two that I can't miss, are you going to be home?" She snapped back, "I am now. Can anything else go wrong?" Lydia smiled and said, "Robert wants to have a baby." Mom just hung up without a response.

The Boss

"Come in. Have a seat", Dr. Foster said with his 'strictly business' tone. Lydia stepped into the boss' office and took a chair next to the window. "Lydia, we both know why you're here. Since you have taken over, your department has developed into a dead-end road. The character and nature of the department is beginning to leach out to other areas and I have been looking for ways to correct it. Do you have the solution?"

"Dr. Foster, I have run both cooperative and non-cooperative Game Theory boards on my entire staff and my department but I keep ending up with only circular theory arguments. I can't seem to establish the binary base. I have begun a game board to self-evaluate my motives and management style and to be completely honest, I think I am the problem."

Dr. Foster just stared for a moment. "Mrs. Jackson, I

believe that is one of the most honest assessments I have ever heard and I know that was difficult for you but, you have not answered my question. Do you have the solution or solutions?"

Lydia was frozen. Taking blame always worked before, she thought to herself, 'he's got to be a republican'. "No sir, I do not. But I will by the time we come back off winter break." thinking she needed to buy some time. She noticed he didn't seem to have a today strategy when he hesitated on his response.

"Mrs. Jackson, do you remember the question I posed to you and the other two candidates for this position and the reason you were chose?"

"Yes sir. 'Three people were at a bus stop and it was raining badly. One was a gorgeous man that I would just love to meet. One was my best friend in college and the other was a very elderly lady with pneumonia, headed for the hospital. I had just bought the car of my dreams and it only had two seats. What would I do?'"

He picked up the story, "And you said, you would let your best friend use your car to assist the elderly woman while you took the bus with the mystery man. Mrs. Jackson, that is why you were hired. You found a way for all four people to win. That is what I want you to do with your department. I am going to give you until February first to change your departments behavior or change your employer."

Lydia stood up, she was not use-to being spoken to in such a manner or tone. It was not just disrespectful but it was rude. Even her father did not speak to her that way. "Is that all sir?"

Dr. Foster stood up and moved closer to her, "Mrs. Jackson, I want you to succeed. I'm going to help you with two formulae and one observation. First, what is the definition of management?" She was positive he could see steam coming from her ears so she just waited. "The definition of management is 'Getting Work Done Through Others.' That does not mean you do their work, in order to win. When you do their work, you create a department that is all about you and you create a staff that always needs your help. Second, please read the plaque on the wall."

Lydia walked over and glance first at the author, Albert Einstein. 'If we don't change our way of thinking, we will not be able to solve the problems that we create ourselves with our current ways of thinking.'

"You see, Mrs. Jackson, the question you were asked upon your employment was a, Game Theory of Social behaviors. Yes, it does demonstrate your problem-solving abilities but I designed it to allow me to see a candidate's method and motives. At first glance, one might think that getting the elderly woman out of the rain was motivated by altruism. Another might see the motive as lasciviousness toward the man. But I saw that you like to win. Every puzzle is about you winning. You are totally self-absorbed, even your excuse for your departments performance was all about you.

Mrs. Jackson, the Congressional Budget Office is not about you. I pray you will have a good Christmas Holiday and are refreshed when you return." He returned to his seat and Lydia didn't need to be shown to the door.

It was all she could do not to slam it as she left. "I can't believe it", she thought, "He just accused me of being narcissistic." She thought about the Social Triangle Theory of power, responsibility and vulnerability' and how he took out a hammer and nail, and nailed all the responses right in the middle of her back. I moved my pawn to the vulnerable position by telling him I was the problem but he wouldn't go for the rescue. He stayed in the power position and would not let me play away from the responsibility position. Damn, he's good, but why am I so mad? She smiled as she though, "God made the earth in six days. I got six weeks, not a problem.

Talk with Mom

Lydia couldn't wait to leave and get to her mom's. She could hear the office party as she stepped off the elevator. She thought, "I'll just stay a few minutes. No one here going anywhere in life but home."

Joanna spotted her and reached out and grabbed her hand, "Mrs. Jackson, you have to hear this." Richard had already drank more than enough and was doing his stand-up comedy routine, "Mrs. Jackson, There was two men lost in a hot air balloon. They came close to the Hart Building and saw a woman standing on the roof. They called to her and asked, 'We are lost. Do you know where we are?' The lady called back, 'You are in a hot air balloon.' They called back down, 'You must be an actuary." The lady asked, 'Yes. Why would you say that?' They replied, 'You just gave us the facts but we are not any better off than before we asked.' The lady called back, 'You must be from marketing.' They said, 'Yes. How did you know?' She said, 'I gave you the facts and now you want to make it my fault.'"

Lydia couldn't help but laugh. The joke wasn't that funny but Richard was so absorbed in it that watching him get a kick, was humorous. "I really have to be going" Lydia said, as she wished everyone a great holiday.

After two hours in traffic, what normally was the calming sight of her mother's driveway now felt like the feeling you get at the top of a rollercoaster. She put the car in park and her mom was already at the door waiting.

"How was work?" she asked as she opened the door for Lydia to come in. "Before or after the letter?" Lydia asked, "Before, it was great. Afterwards, all downhill. Now, why didn't you tell me about the letter?" They sat down in the living room and her mother was noticeably nervous.

"Lydia, I just wasn't sure. To be honest, I'm still not one hundred percent sure about all this." Lydia still was only half in her chair, "Sure about what? You said, 'No, no, no, not the letter', Tell me what you know." "Baby, you are the fourth generation. Grandma Margaret and Grandpa Manoah, both claimed to have been visited by an Angel on top of Cohutta Mountain back in December of 1919.

They claimed the Angel gave them the names and order of four generations of girls and the fourth one was to be named Lydia Fayth and that God had a special purpose for her."

Deannah began to have a nervous shake and Lydia, even though uncomfortable, tried to calm her mother. "But mom, why didn't you tell me about this when I was young?" Deannah stood up and walked to the dining room bay windows and then started reworking the chairs at the table. "Lydia, how was I supposed to know? Me and all three of your grandmothers fought like hell over baby names. Because of the last fight, I almost lost you and I hated Grandma Margaret ever since. We never saw each other after that and I refused to let her see you because of what happened.

Do you remember the story about your birth?" Lydia stood up so she could speak directly to her mother, "You mean about me being premature? I remember bits and pieces." Deannah moved back around the table, taking Lydia by the hand and both sat down on the sofa. "Baby, I'm going to tell you the way I saw it then and the way I see it now.

I took my pregnancy test a couple of days before Christmas and sprang the news on your father as a Christmas present. He was thrilled. He and I started going over boys and girl names. We had settled on a couple and told the family the news at the New Year's Dinner. That is when all hell hit the fan.

Your grandmothers, especially grandma Margaret, were ecstatic. All three of them informed me and your father that it would be a girl and the name would be Lydia Fayth. I had grown up hearing the story about the Angel but Baby, I was born in 57', life was new and full of adventure and growth going on in every direction. The fact was, I never looked at the story as anything more than just an old-folk, tall tale.

Anyway, there were a lot of heated debates, especially from your father. He wasn't having anything to do with it. Well, I went for the sonogram on Valentine Day and it was a girl, which just poured fuel to your grandmothers' fire. The following day I was scheduled for my first exam. Grandma Margaret called and I got way out of hand. After I hung up the phone, my water broke. I was mad and made it to the bed but by that afternoon when your father got home, my water had broken five times.

We made it to the hospital and everything went crazy. I was only at twenty-six weeks of pregnancy and the first specialist that came in must have been on the devil's payroll. He gave you zero chance of living and me only fifty, fifty if I would abort you. In just a few minutes they had to sedate me from trying to kick him out of the room. Finally, my doctor got there and said it was time. The last thing I remember was your father and grandpa Manoah talking. When I woke up the next day, you father had named you.

To this day I don't know for sure if you got a shotgun name or if Grandpa and your father came to a deal of some kind. I blamed everything on grandma Margaret and swore she would never see you. You were thirteen ounces and twelve inches long. The lady doctor said you had no eyes and you would probably never develop them. Every negative thing that could be said from the doctors, was said but I wasn't having any part of it.

You came out of one hundred and twenty days of NICU absolutely, perfect with a complete set of eyes, heart and lungs. That's how I saw it then. But now, I know grandma Margaret wasn't the cause of you coming early. Baby, your mother wasn't a saint when she was young and I've did a lot of things that only God and I know about, but when they told me you were a girl, I knew God had forgiven me and all of hell or grandmothers wasn't taking you from me."

Lydia didn't have much to say, she just leaned over and hugged. She handed her mother the letter and mom read it. She looked up a Lydia and said, "It still feels like they are taking you from me. Baby, I don't know what to tell you. I can say that

I have seen too much to think this couldn't be possible. I will say this, 'Grandma Grace is the executor of South Gate Plantation and she'd know way more about this than I would.'

The plantation is one very, very nice agriculture operation. They didn't trust me to be the executor, they knew I'd sell it out of spite. But I really don't hold any hard feelings toward anyone of them."

Just then the front door opened and Paul came in. Paul was the stepfather and an up-and-coming politician on the national scene. Paul seem to show up right after Lydia's dad died at the pentagon on 9/11, but there was a lot about Paul you wanted to steer clear of. Lydia snickered and asked, "Mom, what did you see in that mafia hit man?" Paul smiled with his come back, "Hey now, that's no way to treat the guy who got you your job." Lydia laughed out loud, " I guess it didn't have anything to do with my degrees?" Paul was in the kitchen by now and shouted back, "This is Washington baby, it's all in how you spin it."

Everybody chuckled as Deannah walked Lydia to the door, "Now, what was this about Robert wanting to have a baby? Tell him to go ahead and have one and call you when it's out of diapers." Lydia skipped the whole subject, "Mom, you've been a manager for ever. What do you tell new managers that are just getting started?"

Deannah looked up to make eye contact, "Lydia, are you having trouble?" Lydia nodded, "Just a few bumps in the road but I still have my hands on the wheel." "Well, Mrs. Jackson", her mother smiled, "I'll tell you what I tell all my managers.

A, B, C, Activate, Behavior, Consequence.

All managers can activate. Activate is setting the goal or target. A, is your job and yours alone. You must know what you want performed, from taking out the trash to a complete project profile report by Friday. First mistake a manager makes is assuming their subordinates understand what they want.

Then B, the subordinate performs the behavior. The manager is graded on how well the desired performance is repeated or ingrained. You have four basic type subordinates, those that know what to do and those that don't and then two subcategories of each, those that want to and those that don't.

The way you manage that is C, Consequence, the manager's response to the performance. This is the part of a manager's job they just leave out. If you assign a task then your job is not completed until you make a response to their behavior. You either, reward or reprimand. Second and most dangerous mistake ninety nine percent of managers do is reprimand and they do that without intelligent design. Even a manager is in one of the four categories and most just don't know how to.

A manager must be aware at all time, that this is what makes a manager, 'You are amplifying or adjusting behavioral performances. ' Only the top one percent of managers spend their days rewarding good behavior. Complimenting good behavior or performance is amplifying the desired behavior.

The manager that wants more good behavior should amplify that behavior by rewarding it and saying so.

When was the last time you told one of your subordinates, 'Job, well done!'?" Lydia thought for a moment, "once or twice last week." Deannah looked at her, "I responded to well over twenty today, separately. Mrs. Jackson, I know you have a well-educated staff.

Are you sure you haven't taken the wind out of their sails by reprimanding more than rewarding? What you speak about, you bring about.

If you are always showing up and speaking negatively, that will be the performance your department will give you more of.

If you fill your department with high fives, well done and way to go's, you will get better performance. You are the head coach, not the head worker.

So, let's review. First, know what you want. Second, Activate the action by assigning it to someone. Put a name on it, not just implying what you would like. Third, let them do the behavior. Keep your hands off. And finally, examine the behavior and reward or adjust to achieve your desired performance."

Lydia just shook her head, "You always make it simple. You are the best teacher on the planet! Love you, Gotta go." They hugged and kissed and she was on her way.

Home

Traffic had calmed down a great deal for the ride home. Lydia was at a stop light when she decided to call. The phone rang and Grandma Grace picked up on the second ring. "Hi Grandma, are you busy? Lydia paused. Oh Lydia, I was thinking about you today. Christmas is just around the corner and I'd like you and that almost good enough husband to plan on spending some time with us." "Grandma, that sounds great but I need to visit with you for a while, this week end, if you're free."

Grace was in full spirit of the season, "Grandpa and I are Christmas shopping tomorrow. Why don't you and Robert spend tomorrow night with us?" "Grandma, I don't think that will work. You know how his Saturdays are spent trying to get ready for Sunday morning broadcasts." "Well then, how about you going to church with us Sunday morning?" Lydia had to stop for another light, "Perfect, I'll be there at eight.

I just left mom's and she said I should talk to you. I got a letter today from Grandma Margaret." Lydia jerked the phone away from her ear, the screaming sound filled the car and seemed to bounce off every glass. When it got quiet, Lydia picked up the phone, she listened intently and she heard what sounded like Grandma Grace running through the house screaming, " *PRAISE GOD! PRAISE GOD, PRAISE GOD!"*

Lydia spoke into the phone, "Grandma? Grandma? Grandma, are you there? Grandma, I'll see you Sunday." Lydia smiled uncontrollably and thought, Grandma Grace always was the excitable kind.

Her phone rang, she answered it, "Grandma?". It was Robert, "Not today I'm not, but give me a few years and we'll see what happens." with a small laugh, "Hey Baby, when you coming home? I stopped and got us something greasy and hot." She thought before she spoke, "Pizza? no, well then, not hamburgers!, no, okay, chicken? I'll be home in about fifteen minutes, I'm passing the post office now." Robert, in his best romantic voice, "Can I start sucking up? I'll start your bath water."

Lydia thought about what her mother just taught her, A, B, C. "Now that's a real man." she said "Sure you can." grinning as she thought about performance enhancement. "Be waiting" Robert said as he hung up.

She thought for a moment and tried to muster up a feeling of guilt. She thought, Lydia, bad girl, go to the end of the line. By the time she pulled into her driveway she thought, Lydia, I thought I told you to go to the end of the line. Why are you back at the front? She spoke to herself out loud, "I went back there but someone had already taken my place, so I just had to come back to the front."

She turned off the car, grabbed her laptop and the letter, hit the garage door button and was headed for a nice warm bath and some greasy chicken.

What He Thinks

Lydia decided not to bring up the letter with Robert until Saturday evening, as to not interfere with his show prep. As the evening was winding down, Lydia started laying out her clothes for church. Robert eyed the outfit she had laid out on her dressing table, "Hey girl! Where are you going, looking so good?" She couldn't help but smile, "Going to church with Grandma Grace in the morning and after lunch, she and I are going to see great grandma Fayth at the retirement community."

"You going to church? What's up?", he said as he was laying out his suit. She took a deep breath and decided to spill the whole story, even though she knew that she didn't need or really want his opinion,

"It seems that we have had a great family secret for four generations and they finally decided to let me in on it. Seems that great, great grandma Margaret and grandpa Manoah were visited by an Angel that told them I was coming and what to name me and that God had a special plan for me." There it was, she, spit it out in two sentences.

Robert had stopped dead in his tracks, holding a belt and a pair of shoes. "Those don't match" Lydia offered as she walked into her closet again. Robert followed her to the door, "Are you serious or are you pulling my leg?" Lydia went to her night stand and handed him the letter, "I received this certified, Friday. I called mom and she lost it in a bad way, she sent me to Grandma Grace and she lost it in a good way and now I'm going to find out what both my grandmothers know about this."

Robert sat on the bed reading the letter. He finally looked up and asked, "Is this for real? I mean, really?" Lydia responded, "You know what I know. Mom said she grew up knowing the story but shrugged it off as folk lore." Robert looked at the envelope, then read the entire letter again, "Is there such a place as South Gate?"

Lydia was still busying about her clothes, "Yeah, our family owns a pretty large farm operation. I looked it up today. For it being in the south, it's pretty high tech., lots of solar stuff operating the green houses and aquaponic fish farming. Seems like grandma Margaret and Grandpa Manoah saw a coming crisis in America and made it their mission to set a model in motion. I feel kinda cheated that I didn't know about all this while I was coming up."

Still analyzing the letter with his journalist instincts, "Baby, I don't know about all this but there may be something to the crisis thing. Have you ever heard about the Dalton Minimum or The Year Without a Summer?"

Lydia thought for a second, "No. Can't say that I have." Robert continued, "Please, when you get a chance, look it up. It was a world-wide cold weather condition between 1790 and 1830. And it was so cold that in 1816 there was no summer!

Snow fell in New York on June 6th and all crops quit growing by July 7th because the ground was frozen."

Lydia looked straight at him, "What exactly does that have to do with me?" Robert was accustomed to all conversations evolving around her, "Well, NASA climatologist have determined that we are at the very beginning of another down turn. Apparently, the global leaders are so sure of it that even Russia is beginning to make moves to secure other resource. I know your consumer data and demographics will alter dramatically at your work and it may tie into this letter."

Lydia hated anything she could not control, "Well, that's just great. God wants me to save the world and he's going to make me cold while I do it. Maybe I should call my broker to invest in wool. It seems every time you and I talk about anything, you shift everything out of my control. It's like, if you can shake my foundation, then you'll be right there to show me how to survive, you'll be the hero! What seems to be your problem? Strong women threaten you?"

Robert threw up his hands in disgust, "It never fails. It's all about you. I'm not saying your weak. How do we end up like this in every real discussion of facts? I share information and you find a way to see it as an attack." Lydia didn't hear a thing past, 'it's all about you'. "That is the second time in two days that a man has accused me of being self-centered. I, had to take it from the boss, but from you I don't. You should start thinking about new arrangements after the first of the year. By the way, when you are making your argument, don't say, 'WE end up'. It is not we, it is you. We do not argue, you do. We did not discuss having a baby, you did."

Robert just stared as Lydia walked out of the room. He folded the letter, placed it back in the envelope and tossed it onto her night stand. He walked to his closet door and thought, "well, I guess this is what it feels light to start over."

Chapter Three

Church

Grandpa John opened the door for Grandma Grace and Lydia to enter the church. We made our way to our seats as grandpa had to talk to every other person along the way. It appeared to be a friendly church, mid to older members. Lydia scanned the parking lot before coming in, mostly, middle income range of cars. She couldn't help herself, she thought, "Maybe I should apply to the FBI or something. I seem to evaluate everything and everybody and I'm good at it."

Grandma Grace had already read the letter and had affirmed the story as absolute fact. Something the whole family knew and agreed on, except mom, but even mom would not discount it as impossible. Grace looked at Lydia, "when are you leaving for South Gate? God, I wish I could see Grandma Margaret again. Lydia, you are one special person and I'm sure your life is going to change a lot. You just hold on to your dreams and you'll make it."

Lydia didn't want to hurt grandma's feeling but, "Grandma, this is more like a nightmare than a dream. My life is in DC., my job, all the years of schooling, everything has led up to my career. This came out of nowhere. This is day three of a tornado and I feel like I'm in a plane with no pilot." Grace smiled as she held Lydia's arm, "Lydia, your mother came up during a time when God was being ran out of school. You were never taught about God. You only got to see back biting and church gossip. Did you ever read the entire Bible?"

Lydia felt a little freer to speak frankly, since she got her first point off her chest, "Of course. Twice but the problem is I still didn't get it. I believe Jesus is the son of God but all else is commentary. Especially the Old Testament but when I was in high school, mom told me that the Old Testament didn't count anymore."

"Well you mother was in error", Grandpa had walked up behind us, unnoticed. "Lydia my child, grandpa has never told you wrong. Listen to me on this." Grandpa had retired a very wealthy DC attorney, "The letter you got is true and you shall soon know it for yourself and this is the way you'll know you're on the right path. Illumination. Most folks call it revelation but It's when you are working on something and God is involved, out of nowhere the information will be delivered to you. Maybe through a stranger, maybe a commercial or a magazine or maybe through the preaching of the word. But when it hits you, the light will go off. That is why the scriptures say, 'those that sat in the valley of the shadow of death, have seen a great light'.

The Holy Spirit's job is to convince, convict and convert. You, are in need of the convincing part." Grace joined in, "We have a very educated preacher here at our church. Who knows? God may speak to you today." Lydia sat back as the choir began the opening hymns and soon the preacher had made it to the podium.

Lydia's mind was on rapid fire, listening half way for a mistake but somewhere hidden deep inside was a wanting, a kinda hopeful looking for the key to unlock the door to this mystery tornado she found herself locked within.

The Preacher didn't appear pretentious or over bearing. He began, fairly, slow and methodical to set the foundation of the message. "It is somewhat difficult, if not nearing impossible for one to understand the Bible, it's stories and people, if one, does not have, an understanding of the word, 'Testament'. Our Bible is made up of two testaments, one that is called old and the other call new. It is unfortunate that most people have no knowledge of the word's meaning or the origin. The word is derived from the word Covenant. God calls it the Old Covenant and the New Covenant. It is God, entering, into covenant with Abram in the Old Covenant and then sending his son, to open up a covenant with us in the New Covenant.

In old times, when men entered, into covenant they would cut their hands and shake hands to join their blood. This was the most sacred relationship one could enter.

Here in America we get to see glimpses of this. From special forces rushing into gunfire to save a covenant brother, to firefighters charging the flames of hell to save a child. From the heroes of 9/11 to patriots and veterans. But it saddens me to say, that here in America, we have fallen away from the knowledge of this most valuable of all constitutions.

In times of old, an Indian male child would have to call all the women in the tribe, mother or sister because it was not acceptable for a male Indian to go to sleep with a hungry mouth in the camp. Now compare this to your town. How about your community? How about your church? Even let us examine this church. Have we entered, into covenant with each other?

I was reading the journals of Pastor Jack Hale, the founder of this covenant body and I found myself convicted by just the reading. Let me share with you a portion of his writing. 'I was visiting with brother and sister Satterfield after the loss of their son in the war. They had a young visitor from Washington DC that said he was a Christian. Brother Satterfield listened to the brother's witness for a few moments and then replied.

"Son, you don't know anything about church. You may know a lot about God but I can tell you know nothing about a covenant church body.

The young visitor was pleasant and even eager to learn. Brother Satterfield said that when he was young, he and his brother would go to the field with their mule. If they heard the church bell ringing, they would straight way, put up the mule and head directly to the church. He asked the young visitor if he knew why. Not knowing, he continued to explain that they were called there to dig a grave. All the men would gather round and dig. Each taking about a one-minute turn on the shovel. He said the kin would come out and lay down their love one and return inside, we would then cover the dead. Know why we did that son? Cause next week it could be one of ours.

Ya'll have lost church and replaced it with clubs.' Now, I would like to share with you a true story that I know firsthand.

A dad worked at night and the mother worked in the morning. When dad got off, he would drive the three little girls to the babysitter so he could sleep for the next nights work. One morning, while driving the girls to the sitter, he dosed off. The truck hit a tree and, the four-year old girl died.

Now, let me ask you this question. Was she guilty of any crime? Was that baby girl innocent? I can tell by your responses that you agree with me that she was and is innocent. That tells me that you have the ability, to judge fairly. Now, let me ask you this, was Jesus guilty? Was he innocent? Please allow me to continue so I may show you the innocent blood of the covenant in which most of you have entered.

In the Old Covenant, Moses took the innocent blood of a lamb and placed it on the door posts and lintel and the Angel of Death would not cross it. All of Heaven and all the devils recognize innocent blood. In the New Covenant, Jesus said, 'this is my blood of the new covenant.

Let me ask you, Are you innocent? Have you ever lied, cheated or even taken the Lord's name in vain? Would the devil recognize your blood as innocent as the four-year old girl's? But Jesus' blood, would it be recognized as innocent as that little girl's? I would say yes. If you could cut your hand and Jesus cut his, would you shake his hand and enter in to a blood covenant with innocents? When we place his blood, his heart upon our hearts, we enter, into the New Covenant.

In conclusion let me draw your attention to a few truths. First, it would be hard, if not impossible to comprehend Old or New Testament, Covenant, absent of a working knowledge of the meaning and manners of the word, 'covenant'. Many, struggle to understand the scriptures or the stories of the Bible. Without the pragmatic outline of covenant, all study of His word would be nothing more than a narcissistic exercise of self-expression.

Secondly, it would appear, that in this, modern day church world, many join the club but very few enter in to covenant with Jesus. This would be of great concern since Jesus said, 'no one can come unto the Father except by me.' and also, 'if you will not take of this cup, you'll have no part with me.'

Thirdly, I would ask that each of us, as members of this body, ask the Lord how we are to re-establish the covenant body. It would appear, that if an Indian tribe would take care of its own, those of us in covenant with the Son of God, should take care of our own.

This is not an invitation to become a do-good rescuer. Money and help of any kind is an amplifier. If you help or give money to a good person, you will have amplified their ability to be and do more good. In the same manner, if you help a person of poor choices or destructive habits, you have amplified that in both their lives and your community.

And God requires us to tend his garden. It is said that if you give a man a fish, you have fed him for a day. But if you teach him to fish, you have feed him for life. However, I say, if you give a man a fish, without requiring him to learn to fish, you have made him dependent for life. There is no greater harm to man, than helping him out of the cocoons he has woven for himself. You may equip him with the knowledge and skills to break free but never do it for him. Never become the rescuer. If you do so, he will never be free.

And finally, there are many people that believe Jesus is the son of God but have not entered, into a covenant. Jesus, by himself has made a way for you to enter, into covenant with him. He has given you the freedom and tools to break free from whatever cocoon you are wrapped up in. Whether it is your body with sickness, your soul with disease or your spirit with narcissistic apathy."

Lydia's mind was trying to retain all the tiny particles of every sentence. It was too much, her mind imagined a game board matrix where she could accurately cross examine each piece of evidence. But she got hung up in space and time at several points. When he mentioned 9/11, she became suspended there for a brief, moment. Lydia lost her dad at the Pentagon on 9/11. She was 19 at the time and two years ran through the filing cabinet of her head, but by the time he dropped the 'narcissistic' bomb, she had already dropped her defense shield and her heart was fragmented.

Grace looked at her and began, "Well, preacher was a little on the dry side today." Lydia's spirit turned a complete back flip, she couldn't believe what she just heard from grandma. She though, there is no way she just said that. I got the whole thing.

She had this inner urge to be alone, maybe for an hour or so, just to digest or categorize her knew understandings and how they would apply to her. She didn't talk much on the ride back, she just put her mind on auto pilot. It seemed as if the tornado had slowed down to a Sunday pace.

Great Grandma Fayth

Great grandma Fayth was born in 1920, the year following Margaret Ann's visit from the Angel. Needless, to say, Mrs. Brigit Fayth Trotter had a regal air about her that demanded attention and respect. She wasn't difficult or demanding, quite the contrary. She grew up on the farm and she was the one responsible for converting the operation to an educational plantation. She was, or should I say, still is an exuberant teacher. If you are going to be around her, you are going to learn something, or should I say, a dozen things before you leave.

Even though I had not spent any time with grandma Fayth while I was growing up, she was always my favorite at the family reunions each year. I knew if I was going to believe this story and the fact that the letter said that Grandma Margaret and Grandpa Manoah would come back themselves and teach me, it would have to come from Grandma Fayth.

The drive was about an hour after we ate lunch and I saw the retirement community up ahead. Grandpa John said he would drop us off and he would do a little Christmas shopping in the small tourist town, just up the road. When grandpa told the security guard at the gate, who we were there to see, the older gentleman chuckled and asked, "Sure you're up for it?" We all laughed as we drove away and continued around the well-maintained clubhouse and pond. We stepped out of the car and the small tingle of winter air reminded us to button up.

Grandma Grace and I started walking toward the clubhouse but, heard the sound of laughter coming from near the pond. Grandma Grace looked at me and smiled, "Bet that's Fayth." We made our way down a cypress tree lined walkway and saw a small group of older women sitting near the water. They were laughing and snorting and seemingly impervious to the fact that we were close enough to listen.

"Listen, you just write it like I tell you and it will work. Okay, write, 'Tall slender mature woman who can still cook frog legs and squirrel, between the ages of OMG and OTH, looking for mature man who doesn't drool, to take short strolls in the moonlight and enjoys old movies. You got that all down?" By that time, everybody was rolling in laughter, that is, except the lady writing it all down. "Excuse me ladies", Grace interjected.

"Grace!" exclaimed grandma Fayth as she ran around the table and was meet with Grace screaming and hugging. "Fayth, she got the letter!" Grandma Fayth stood frozen like she had been shot. It startled the group of ladies, who all quickly gathered around her. They sat Fayth down at the table, her eyes never leaving Lydia.

"Come here child", she said with a smile. "Ladies, this is my great, great granddaughter that I have told you so much about." As Lydia came close and joined Fayth in hugs, the ladies stood back, almost in a reverence type atmosphere. "Lydia, there has not been a day in my life that I have not prayed for you. I have told the entire story to so many people in my life, these ladies have heard it hundreds of times. Mom's, dad's and my entire life was spent preparing for your coming and from the day you were born until now it has been praying for your success and protection. And now you're here. The day foretold has dawned upon us while we played. I feel ashamed."

Lydia hugged her again, "Grandma, you're probably not going to have time for that. I really need your help sorting through all this, I seriously have not been prepared for this, nor did I know anything about it." Fayth made eye contact, "You really didn't know?" "No Ma'am. Not a clue until Friday's certified letter", Lydia reached up to touch the hand of grandma Grace who had just placed her hands upon Lydia's shoulder, which lightened the mood slightly.

Fayth smiled up at Grace, "I guess the girl has a lot of questions. You brought her to the right place." Lydia wanted to get grandma Fayth back in her element so she started her questions, "Grandma, one question comes to mind at the top of the list." Fayth looked serious, prepared to answer anything like being on the witness stand, "Yes, child?"

Lydia asked, "What does OMG and OTH mean?" Fayth and the ladies broke out in laughter again, " Oh My God and

Over the Hill." "But grandma, running an ad in the personals?" Fayth could hardly contain herself long enough to respond, "Child, you try spending every weekend watching TV with a bunch of old women who smell like bengay and witch hazel. Anyway, they'd end up over at my place watching John Wayne." At that, everyone got up laughing and headed back to the clubhouse.

Once things settled in to 'whatever' was normal with eighty and ninety-year olds, Fayth's living room was packed. Wasn't anyone going to gossip about this, they were all first-hand listeners. Fayth made sure everyone had tea and then stood up and asked everyone to bow their heads in prayer.

"Lord, we are here. It is time. Strengthen us all for our parts and prepare the Watchman at the South Gate. Amen"

She looked at Lydia and Grace, "There isn't any need in retelling the story, everyone here has heard it many times. They are here to witness for themselves the words that have been foretold. I am here to answer for you, anything I can and to prepare you if there is a need. What can I do?"

Lydia had somehow, over the passed three days, become immune to feeling uncomfortable, insane was becoming the new norm so she just plunged in, "I hate to rain on the parade but this is not normal. God shows up and tells your mom and dad to name four consecutive girls and then the last one will be Lydia Fayth. Will you explain that to me please? And while you're at it, can you tell me what your father said to mine that convinced him to name me that?"

Fayth didn't miss a beat, "Sure can. You're right. It is not normal. Sorry, God doesn't have an excuse for that. It is his habit. As for the names, Brigit Fayth, Brigit Grace, Deannah Brigit and Lydia Fayth.

Each name has special meanings, in and of themselves. First thing you should note is that each of your mothers are career teachers. That is what we do. Also notice the way the names are put together.

Brigit is first in mine and Grace's but placed second in your mother's. That is the character and nature of that person. The bridge is the character in my life and faith is my nature. The bridge was first with Grace and grace is her nature. The name Deannah means teacher and she placed teaching first, that is her character and the bridge is her nature. Then Lydia means trust, which is your character and faith will be your nature. This has been God's way from the beginning.

In the beginning, with Adam, He allowed Adam to name all things and what so ever, 'shame' Adam gave them, that is what they were called. The Hebrew word 'shame' means, character and nature. Just like a fruit tree, it's nature is to bear fruit but the characteristics of fruit trees vary greatly.

Everywhere God wants something to change, He does it with a name, Abram to Abraham, Jacob to Israel. The etymology of names in the bible draw a vivid full color picture of God in action. Look at Matthew chapter one. Look up the meaning of the names and write them down and you will see a pictorial graph of redemption. Now, does God hide women in His word in such a way to speak to us in due season? In Matthew chapter one there are four women in the lineage of the Christ. Women are never listed in a lineage in a man's world so they must be there for a reason. Let's look closer, these four women are gentile women, they would never be listed in a

Hebrew, man's world lineage. So, there must be, therefore, a reason.

They were, Tamar, Rehab, Ruth and Bathsheba. And when you look at their 'shame', character and nature, you see the identical pattern of the four generations it took to get you here. Tamar had a secret place, Rehab had faith, Ruth found grace and Bathsheba was obedient.

While we are on names let's look at mom's, Margaret Ann Elbertson. Margaret means, 'child of light', Ann means, 'favor and grace' and the name Elbertson, given to her upon marriage means, 'magical or noble power'.

God has built three bridges to get you here and what you have now heard is just a fraction of what is in the diaries. Momma could teach us from them but we could never see them. She was strict about that, she said they were for you to get and then they could be seen and shared but not until. I made myself, God and momma a promise, 'I would not leave this earth until I laid my hands upon those precious books with you safe' and I intend to keep that promise!"

Upon the word 'diaries', the room got real, quiet, it was like magic filled the room. Fayth pause only for a second or two, "What was your other question? Oh yeah, my dad and your dad. The morning before your birth, your mother and mom had it out over the phone. We knew your name and they were not buying it. After they hung up, mom asked dad if he would talk to your dad. That night, Deannah was in the hospital and you were not going to make it. Your father was a military guy and had a lot of respect for Manoah. You see, my dad was a war hero and a prophet, but he never told anyone about all the missions and medals. But your dad worked in the Pentagon and accessed dad's military records. After that, the sun rose and set by dad's opinion, as far as your father was concerned. Manoah never got into the women's argument over the baby name. Deannah was sedated and her doctor told your father that there wasn't any way you were going to make it. Your father turned to dad and asked what to do.

Dad said, 'name the child Lydia Fayth and she will live', and that's what he did and that is why you are here."

Fayth went to a chair to sit down, Lydia looked at grandma Grace and then back to grandma Fayth. Lydia seemed to just surrender inside, it was kind of like drowning. Day after day, one wave after another coming over you until surrendering is what you want. You know surrendering doesn't mean peace, quite the opposite, it means that I have crossed a rope bridge and cut the ropes so there is no going back. Whatever lies ahead, I'll have to deal with it, but at least my body is not in one world and my head in another.

Suddenly Grandma Fayth leaned over, the ladies jumped into action. She said, "I'm having trouble breathing. Feels like the devil is sitting on my chest." One of the ladies hit the red button beside the phone. Within minutes there were paramedics and staff all over the place. All the way to the hospital, grandma Fayth held my hands. You could hardly hear her through the oxygen mask, "Lydia, Lydia. I'll be waiting to touch those diaries. Please child, I'll be waiting." The paramedic told me she shouldn't talk. We arrived and they rolled her through those double doors and I just stood and stared.

Hospital

Grandpa John had arrived and we all packed the waiting room. Several hours passed. It was well into the night when the doctors came in. He asked for the family to step outside with them. I looked around at the faces of all her friends and the morning message about covenant flash back across my mind,

"We are all family. Just tell us all." "Hi, my name is Dr. Archer and this is Dr. Soteria. Mrs. Trotter is in ICU and is doing well for her age. We had to remove a blood clot from her main artery and the procedure went well. However, with her age, we will have to watch her for several days to see if any more clots approach her heart. If all goes well, we might get her out by Christmas day."

As we thanked them, I noticed the ladies from the retirement community were huddled over in a corner and seemed to be having a discussion. I moved right in, "what is it?" The lady that was writing for grandmother earlier in the day, spoke up, The doctor's names. Did you notice? Archer and Soteria?" I was not in critical thinking mode, "I missed it." She said, "in your story, 'the Lord's Archer' and soteria is a Greek word for Salvation of the Lord." Another lady spoke up, "He sent his word and healed them." Then another, "Death and life are in the power of the tongue, those that love it shall eat the fruit there of." Then it became infectious as the ladies and a few of the older men started firing the arrows of the Lord back and forth, "By your words you shall be justified and by your words you shall be condemned, The sower soweth the word, By his

64

stripes we were healed, You have not because you ask not, Ask and you shall receive, seek and you shall find, knock and the door shall be opened unto you, and, Whosoever shall say unto this mountain, be thou remove and be thou cast into the sea and shall not doubt in his heart but believe those things which he saith shall come to pass, he shall have whatsoever he saith. So, when you pray, believe that you receive and you shall have . . ."

Grace came up, "Lydia, we can see her for just a few moments." We entered the room and she turned her head to see us and reached for me, "Lydia, so much I want to teach you but Mom and Dad are waiting on you." Lydia had tears coming down her cheeks. She thought, it was her Dad's funeral the last time she felt tears and that was ten years ago. "Grandma, I want to stay with you." Fayth motioned for Grace and John to come closer,

"The South Gate will only open for three days and it will be closed for another seven years. It has been ninety-one years since the Angel, which is seventeen cycles of seven. Lydia is twenty-nine, the same age as Jesus when He went to the wilderness. She will only get this one chance for the heavens to open unto her. She must be there by December twenty first to get prepared. Ryan will be her guide and Elizabeth will tend her needs."

Just then the alarms went off and nurses came pouring in. They rushed us out and I saw Dr. Soteria running in the door as Grandpa armed Grace and me into the elevator.

Chapter Four

The Drive

It had been a very long night at the hospital but Grandma Fayth was stable and stubborn. She did everything but kick me to make me leave. I arrived back home around ten in the morning and rushed in to pack a few things. Several times, I remember it being said that I had to choose, of my own free will, to go to South Gate. As I was packing my bags, I wondered what that meant. I had developed more than just a simple curiosity but there was almost a sense of belonging. It was like being caught by some unseen force and it was dragging me toward a destiny, somehow attached within me, beneath my emotions and thoughts.

I glanced in Robert's closet. He had several empty boxes piled up in the corner. I recalled his words that said I was self-centered. I thought for a moment, if this letter and visit to South Gate turns out to be real, boy will he be sorry. He'll wish he treated me better.

As Lydia passed through the kitchen, carrying her last bag to the car, she looked at the white board on the fridge. She paused for a moment, grabbed the marker and wrote, 'Gone to South Gate', in all caps.

Once in the car, she typed the address into her GPS and turned toward the interstate headed south, 625 miles, nine hours, thirty minutes, route 66 west to Strasburg, then I-18 south all the way, she read the screen. Easy enough, she thought, only two roads all the way. She stopped just before getting on the Interstate to fuel up and grab some snacks. She glanced at the phone number grandma Grace gave her to call when she got into the town called Ellijay, Georgia, then spoke to herself as she drove up to the toll booth, "I guess I'm really going to do this!"

Time seemed to fly by once she got off the toll road. Sights, sounds and smells of small town life peppered the landscape with glimpses of history as she headed south. She thought back through her American History classes and how her father would rant about the destruction of American freedoms and morals. And how the government was destroying the constitution and the people. That is where she first saw a matrix used to map out social engineering. How welfare actually, hurt the very ones it tried to help and grew poverty instead of reducing it. He use-to look at me and say, "Girl, whatever you do, be a part of the solution!"

She thought how that saying was a major part of her career in government. She wondered if what she was headed to would make her father proud. He was very proud of Manoah, according to Grandma Fayth. It didn't seem to be that long of a drive and before she knew it she saw a sign, 'Ellijay 32 miles'. She looked at her watch, it was 8:54 pm, suddenly she slams on the brakes and the car slid to a stop. Right in the middle of the road stood a deer. She had only glanced at her watch for a second but it was long enough for her to now be sitting sideways in the road, staring at a long drop off a mountain side. The deer bounded up the mountain on the high side, leaving Lydia shaking, she backed up the car to get on her side of the road and drove slowly for the next few miles.

As she drove into the town, fast food caught her eye. Great, she thought, something greasy and this time, southern fried. She turned in and grabbed the paper with Ryan's number. After finishing one fine meal, she looked at the phone number and then at her watch. She really didn't feel like having to meet new people tonight, glancing across the road, she saw a motel. Deciding to brave her first encounter with the South Gate Plantation in the daylight, she drove over to camp out in the solitude of a sixty-dollar room.

Moonset Sunrise

Knock, knock, knock. Knock! Knock! KNOCK! Lydia bounced up in the bed, "Who's There? Wait a minute!" Grabbing her gown and stuffing her sockless feet into cold sneakers, she scrambled for the door. "Who is it?" "Ryan Elbertson ma'am. Are you up?" Lydia spotted the clock, 6:32, "I am now", as she opened the door. "Ma'am, you just gotta see this! Elizabeth sent me to get you but you just gotta see this." Ryan was excited to say the least.

Ryan was a tall muscular young man with jeans and boots. Dark hair, cut neat and somewhat short with a ball cap. His sparkling brown eyes and country boy smile complimented his excited nature and gave Lydia the feeling as if she had known him all her life.

"Ryan, slow down. What are you talking about?" Lydia began getting caught up in his exuberance and had broken out a smile. Ryan was pointing to the horizon, "The Moon, Ma'am. The Moon. Just look at that Moon. Isn't she a beauty?" Lydia looked out at the mountain tops, "Wow! Ryan, Wow! That is worth getting up! I have never seen a full moon so big! I mean, it's bigger than that mountain. It looks so close to us, if we could get to the top of that mountain, we could touch it!" "That's not the half of it ma'am. This only happens about every seven years but this particular-moon, is at the lowest point of the arms and hands and that only happens every ninety-one years. But that's not all, today the sunrise is at 7:41AM and the moon sets at 7:56AM and if that wasn't enough, the sun is with the Archer."

Lydia heard every word but, at the same time, couldn't take her eyes off the moon. "Really, I've never seen anything like it! What mountain is that?" she asked. "That's Cohutta Mountain ma'am. That's where Manoah and Margaret prayed.

Grab some clothes and come out to watch the sunrise." Lydia dashed back in the room and grabbed her clothes. Absorbed by the sites and excitement, she was out the door in under two minutes, with coat, hat and scarf. Lydia walked over to where Ryan was standing. Ryan dropped the tailgate on his jacked-up four-wheel drive truck. It was still too high for Lydia but seemingly without thought, Ryan grabbed her by the waist and seated her on the tailgate.

Lydia didn't know whether to slap him or just get mad but Ryan was oblivious to any wrong doing and bounced up on the tailgate right beside her. Lydia though, He doesn't have a clue that you don't handle a woman that way. Especially one you don't know. She looked at the way he was swinging his legs and imagined him as a little brother, just a clueless one.

"You said your name is Ryan Elbertson?" she asked. "Yes ma'am." She continued, "Any relation to Manoah Elbertson?" He was still swinging his legs, staring at the moon,

"Yes ma'am. Great, great, great uncle. My triple great grandpa's brother." She looked back up at the moon, "Outstanding! You said it is called Cohutta, what's that mean?" He never looked, just said, "It's Cherokee Indian for, 'Tumbling Waters'." I continued, "You said something about the moon being in the arms and hands, mind explaining that?"

He pointed at the moon, "most folks have no idea how important that position of the moon is. Folks in the mountains still do most everything by the signs. You folks call it the zodiac man." He looked at Lydia, "How many degrees are in a circle?" Without thought she responded, "360" but then she thought, "boy, you are way out of your league. Ryan continued, "There are twelve signs so that gives each sign thirty degrees. If the moon was at one degree in Gemini, the man would have his hand raising, but that moon is at twenty-nine degrees Gemini so the man of heaven is lowered his hand down to touch the ground! You see, in December, the full moon is always in the arms and hands but only every ninety-one years does he reach down and touch the mountain. Tomorrow and Thursday the moon will be in the chest but Christmas Eve and Christmas it will enter the heart, what you call Leo." Lydia hung on every word because this boy was way too young to know this, but at the same time her educated side was formulating equations all of which was above her skill set.

She questioned, "I thought astrology and the Bible don't mix. How do you know so much about the moon?" Ryan didn't recognize Lydia's theological debate. He just grew up in the mountains and was raise with and by the round calendar. "I just know what I know. Jesus condemned the Pharisees because they could not discern the signs of the times and God jumped all over Job in chapter thirty-eight for not knowing the twelve zodiacs and the one hundred and forty-four constellations. You should read verses thirty-one through thirty-three. In verse thirty-two, God uses the word 'Mazzaroth'. There is only one definition for the word. The zodiac and the one hundred and forty-four constellations. Then if that isn't enough, the wise men that brought gifts to Jesus, the Greek word for wise is 'magi'. Which only has one definition, 'astrologers'."

"I don't study all the folks in history that make up their minds that this is right and that is wrong. I just study the Word and let Him tell me what He wants. I don't see how all them educated smart people read the Bible. Over two thirds of the Holy Word, were written by astrologers so, unless you know a little about it, you can't even understand what they meant. Like, 'the sky proclaims the work of his hands' or 'for everything there is a time and a season', and the four horses in Revelations, they are the four royal stars of heaven, needless to say I could go on and on."

"Look!" Just then he pointed to the east. "The archer is bringing the sun." Lydia sat there for almost an hour, watching the sun rising on her right hand and the moon disappearing behind the mountain on her left. She had never seen anything like it and according to Ryan, probably would never again in that same way.

"Ryan", Lydia asked, "How did you know I was at the motel?" He smiled as he hopped down off the tailgate, "Ma'am, not many people have a license plate that says, 'CBO.gov', anyway, Mrs. Grace call Mrs. Elizabeth and told us to be expecting you around dark. When you didn't call, Mrs. Elizabeth sent me hunting. Mrs. Elizabeth will be waiting on us.

If you will follow me, I'll show you to South Gate." At that, Lydia loaded her night bag into the car and tagged along the twisting mountain roads.

South Gate Plantation

Ryan stopped his truck in the middle of the road as we came upon two men working on a tractor. He spoke with them for a moment and walked back to me. "Mrs. Lydia, I need to run down to the barn for some tools, if you keep driving around the next curve, you'll see the driveway on your left. Mrs. Elizabeth is waiting on you. I'll catch up with you this afternoon. If you need me before then, Mrs. Elizabeth will call me."

I drove around the truck looking for the curve he spoke of. Driving around the curve was like entering a magical wonderland. One minute you're on a country road, natural and undisturbed, then you round a curve and are struck with the site of manicured evergreens, with a stately entrance. Large stone columns and planters, huge rod iron gates with the letters, 'SG' inlaid and antique octagon pavers lead from the road to a circular driveway.

I stepped out of the car and my eyes locked on to the water fountain in the center of the drive that created what appeared to be an eight-foot sundial and surrounding the water was four-foot high concrete angels of differing poses. The garden and walkways were interlaced with some sort of pattern but from the driveway I couldn't discern what it was.

"Mrs. Lydia, Mrs. Lydia, up here." I turned to look and

standing on the balcony over the front doors was who I assumed to be Elizabeth. "I'll be right down." she called. The house was one hundred percent, southern colonial from pillar to post. I didn't know much about the taste of grandma Margaret but I could tell, this had Grandma Fayth written all over it. Excellence and style. Four great columns graced the double leaded glass doors which had a balcony above which also had double leaded glass doors with a full radius window above. Made you think of a governor's mansion. Once your eye was released from the fountain, the grandeur of the surrounding landscapes commanded your attention to the front door. By the time my eyes made it back to the doors, they opened and out came Elizabeth with a teenage boy and girl.

"Get Mrs. Lydia's things and carry them to her room. "Mrs. Lydia, this is Kevin and Katrina, they are doing their internship here at the plantation for college. All the other students have gone home for the holidays. We normally have twenty or thirty here all year. Kevin and Katrina chose to stay here to help you. We are all so excited, we have been up most of the night waiting on you. When you didn't come in last night like Mrs. Grace said, we called out the posse."

"I apologize. I did not want to disturb anyone after dark", I replied. "Oh Mrs. Lydia! This place was built for you, because of you and belongs to you! Who are you disturbing?" Elizabeth responded in a distinct southern accent, as if I had been joking, then turned to lead me into the house. I paused to look around at the entrance garden and back to the house once more. I thought about how I was apprehensive about coming because the word, 'plantation' conjured up images of old falling down barns and a cold drafty house.

As I walked onto the slate stoned porch, the smell of the fresh cut cypress garland hanging over the entrance, spoke a powerful welcome. I stepped into the foyer and an overwhelming sense of history rose up around me. I looked at the dark rich hardwood floors, then at the enormous gloss white trim that outlined the ten-foot ceilings with a majestic staircase leading to the second floor.

"Mrs. Lydia, let me show you around. This is the dining room to the left." as she opened a set of double doors. "Now, this room to the right is what we call the Bible room. In most homes it would be call a study. But as soon as I open the doors, you'll see why." Elizabeth opened the double stained-glass doors to reveal an immense sea of glass. "Oh my God!" I couldn't believe my eyes. It was a formal living room with white carpet, gorgeous Queen Ann furniture and display cabinets everywhere. Not crowded but extremely full, the corner displays were head high and lighting and glass shelves. Smaller displays were end tables and coffee tables. A set of hand carved, stone tablets of the ten commandments were on the wall behind the love seat on the farthest wall from the door.

"What's that lovely smell?" I couldn't help but ask. "Almond" Elizabeth said while re-adjusting a pearled nativity scene that adorned the coffee table in the center of the room. "God asked Jeremiah, 'What do you see?' Jeremiah said, 'I see the rod of an almond tree, budding and bearing fruit in the middle of winter.' God said, 'You have seen well. I will hasten my word to perform it.' Mrs. Fayth said that was her father's favorite quote and the room has smelled like this from the day it was built." Elizabeth went to the door and waited. The room was so full of beautiful items and I was sure that each one of them wanted to speak to me just like the angel in my certified letter, it was hard to close the doors behind me. I was coming back here tonight!

I don't know how to describe what I was feeling. It was like going through your grandmother's attic on a treasure hunt but this time, I'm going through the whole house and I have a guide. "This is the great room" Elizabeth raising her right arm in tour guide fashion. Her smile gave away the fact that she must like this room a lot. It was considerably large and the fireplace looked a bit peculiar, place in the center stone wall. I had to ask, "Elizabeth, what type fireplace is that?"

Just then, Kevin came into the room. "Kevin, explain the heating system to Mrs. Lydia", Elizabeth smiling like she knew something special. Kevin went over to the small opening and pointed, "This is a rocket heater. This small opening is where we build a fire when needed, which isn't often. Notice how warm the house is now? That is because of the special way the exhaust is ran through this stone wall. The exhaust pipe transfers the heat to the rocks and the rocks heat every room in the house like a radiator. This rock wall goes all the way through the floor to the rooms upstairs and then the exhaust exit's the side wall on the east end of the house. A normal fireplace will use twenty cords of wood a winter to heat a house and will do that very poorly. A wood heater or wood stove will use about ten cords a winter but we heat five thousand square feet with under three cords of wood a winter."

My goodness Kevin, how can that be? You don't use any fans or other heaters on colder nights?" I just couldn't wrap my mind around how this worked. "No, Ma'am. Let me show you. Once the fire is started, it will heat this rock. Imagine putting this one rock into a fire and getting it hot. It would be like a thousand-watt electric heater. Each rock is a heater by its self. Now, look at how many rocks we have just in this room. It's like having two hundred heaters just in here. The coldest time, in the twenty-four-hour cycle is around 6AM. We build a fire right before going to bed and that's it, about seven small logs. Sometimes if we have two or three days with the temperature in the teens, we build another fire midday but that is seldom. The house, livestock housing and greenhouse are all heated with rocket heaters. Even our solar water heater has a rocket back up for winter."

I sniffed to see if I could smell the fireplace. I didn't notice any burnt odor. "Won't smell it either.", Elizabeth was quick to catch on. "That is why it is called a rocket. It draws air through that small fire box so all the smell goes out the exhaust as well. It actually sucks air when the fire is going."

As I looked around the room, my preconceptions of standards were finally dismantled. "I guess I have been in the city to long." everyone chuckled. I looked at the far wall, there was a large portrait, I walked closer and Elizabeth followed. "That is Mr. and Mrs. Elbertson, ma'am." Elizabeth spoke gently. The canvas painting must have been when she was in her thirties, I thought. Very refined autumn tan rancher's overcoat, with her hair well placed under a winter scarf. Manoah had the countenance of a southern statesman with a tall slender build. They were standing in front of a magnificent garden with a gorgeous white Queen Ann greenhouse, accented with black rod iron trimmings and huge coach lanterns hung at the entrance.

"Where was this portrait done?" I asked Elizabeth.

"Come with me and I'll show you the greenhouse." she replied. As we walked through the kitchen, Elizabeth asked Katrina, "We're going to the greenhouse. Want to come?" With a bubbly smile she said, "Oh Yeah!" as she bounced from behind the counter to grab the door for us.

Every door was a pathway to a new adventure. As we stepped out on to the deck, or should I say, "decks?" It reminded me of a cruise ship with multiple decks, bold striking handrails and private seating areas. The landscape was placed in such a way that every deck was bordered with trees and arbors with well, manicured vines that created the atmosphere of an oasis.

As we walked from deck to deck, Katrina described the edible landscape design. "Edible?" I questioned. "Oh yes ma'am. These three trees are figs and they bear in July and this vine is a scuppernong and it bears in September, and of course, my favorite, these are Rainier Cherries. But God needs to fix them." "Fix them? What's wrong with them?" I quickly was concerned. She and Elizabeth began to laugh. "I want Him to make them bear every month but He hasn't arranged that for me yet." I joined into the laughter.

As we rounded the corner of the lower deck and turned to go down the last three steps, there it was. Absolutely breath taking. I stopped in my tracks and just stared, trying to absorb the magnitude of what I was looking at. Just like in the portrait, coach lanterns lined the walkways. Ponds, fountains of various sizes, statues, raised beds and trellises all seemed to point the way to the glass entrance. "Is it just me or is it getting warmer?" I thought that I was reacting to the moment. Katrina, grinning from ear to ear, spoke up, "No ma'am. We are on the east side of the house." I looked at Elizabeth thinking it might be another of Katrina's humors. "She's telling you the truth. Remember Kevin telling you that the heater's exhaust exited on the east side of the house?" I nodded. "That passes through a rock bed under the decks in order to make it more pleasant on the decks in cooler weather.

Also, the sun rises in the east. Notice the house is on a hill and the greenhouse is lower and on the east side of the house. This is to protect it from the bad weather that comes from the northwest and so it will get the sunlight first in the morning but is shaded from sunburn by the hot afternoons in summer." I just shook my head in the wonder of it all.

"Grandma and Grandpa must have been extraordinary", I said, "Do you know much about them?" Elizabeth and Katrina looked at each other and then at me. "Mrs. Lydia, I know what I have been told by Mrs. Fayth and Mrs. Grace. Mrs. Fayth changed my diapers and Mrs. Grace, quite often paddled my behind for breaking limbs in the fruit trees when I climbed them as a kid. I know when I look at you, I am looking at the reason this farm is here and I can't tell you how happy I am inside. To be here when you get to receive the most precious gift the world has ever known since Jesus,"

Elizabeth started tearing up, "my entire life I dreamed of meeting you." Before I knew it, she was hugging me. I thought about my secretary's hug in the office before I left work. It didn't feel the same, I just embraced Elizabeth and somehow lost my professional distance at the same time. "Now, let's go in the greenhouse and pick lunch." Katrina seeming to sense the need to save me. And so, we did, for two hours!

Getting Prepared

I sat watching the sunset from the balcony off my room. I guess it was starting to sink in that I really was here to somehow, meet my grandparents who built this place. It still seemed unbelievable but then, so was this place. Elizabeth set our meeting with Ryan at six and it was now around five thirty. I heard his truck pulling into the front drive. I walked around the balcony to the front and he waved as he made his way to the door.

Once down stairs, Kevin made that little fire and I watched in amazement as to how little effort it took to heat this lovely mansion. Elizabeth asked, "Is it okay if Kevin and Katrina are here?" I was quickened by the question and without effort, transformed back into my managerial character. "I would like to have them stay." I thought it would be helpful to watch the responses of the less informed and balance it off the overly informed because I was beginning to feel less and less like a chosen one and more like a guinea pig.

Elizabeth asked, "Mrs. Lydia, do you have any idea how to open the South Gate of Heaven?" So much for my professional demeanor, "I'm clueless!" Elizabeth walked into the Bible room and returned with two envelopes, "I was told to give you these. They are letters from your grandmother and grandfather. They were left for you in the 1892 family Bible."

I opened Grandma Margaret's and read out loud, "Lydia my dear Angel, if your reading this, I will be seeing you tomorrow. I would like you to see something special in the morning. Would you please watch the sunrise from the top of

Cohutta Mountain? You will be above the clouds and it is a special place. Manoah says that the sunrise is a diamond that man cannot buy, but you can wear it all day, if you see it. While you are there, Manoah will teach you about prayer and I'll be waiting for you in the greenhouse when you return, that is, if you open the gate. Listen for Manoah. Love Grandma Margaret."

Ryan spoke up, "No problem. But I sure am glad it wasn't two weeks ago. We were iced in from the twelfth to the seventeenth. But we're pushing seventy for the high tomorrow." Elizabeth interjected, "God is opening up heaven. He has warmed it up for Lydia. God always operated that way in scripture. Now Ryan, don't you let her out of your sight. You know the mountain, she doesn't."

I looked over at Kevin and Katrina. They appeared to believe every word. I looked back at Elizabeth and then to Ryan, there wasn't an unbeliever in the house. That is, except me. I had to speak up, "I have been trying not to doubt but none of this adds up. I live by numbers and my ability to evaluate facts. If I were capable of establishing an equation for the likelihood of this being possible it would be in the tens of millions."

Ryan laughed, which did not go over well with me. I thought, 'another smartass man child.' "What are you laughing at?" I snapped. "Actually, forty million to one odds! That was the odds of the birth chart of Jesus as calculated by the Tibet wise men who came to give gifts to the new born king. The Bible says, 'God is able to do exceedingly, abundantly, above all, you can ask or think.' You are trying to rationalize and the word for doubt in scriptures is, 'diakrino' which means to separate in thought, or ration thought, i.e., rationalize. What are the odds or equation for God raising Jesus from the dead? Do you think what you have been told is too hard for God?"

By now I was steaming. If he worked for me, I'd fire him and make him like it! I knew I had to keep my professional face on. "Well, maybe you can open South Gate. You seem to have all the answers." "Ma'am. I really don't have a dog in this fight. I have nothing to gain. I'm here because of the family name and your unbelief will not hurt that a bit. You have better odds of meeting a bear on that mountain than your grandparents. But we are not here for me to put bear skins on the wall, we are here to help you. Something you need a lot of.

You are too big for your britches when it comes to the things of God. Let me help your rational mind. The Bible says the wise men came from the east. Due east of Bethlehem is the Tibet Plateau. The latitude for Bethlehem is 32 degrees north. The latitude for Cohutta is 34 degrees north, what's the odds on that?

Elizabeth was getting uncomfortable, as well as Kevin and Katrina. "Ryan, we are here to help her. Can you tell us something constructive?" Elizabeth was better than I thought with her leadership skills.

Ryan looked straight at me as he stood up, "Nope. Unbelief is unbelief. I can't help with that. All I can do is hold up a mirror to it. Mrs. Lydia, I mean you no harm and my desire for you is for you to do God's will. But you will not be able to accomplish that in a state of sin."

I couldn't hold it in any longer, "Let me tell you one thing. You may know a lot but there is one thing you can't say and that is I've done anything wrong here!"

Ryan was non-emotional and continued, "Ma'am, I was not talking about an act of sin. I was speaking about the heart of sin. The doctrine of original sin is best understood as the 'Self Intending Nature, 'S.I.N.' that man was born with. Self-centered, self-right, self-adjusting, self, self, self. Mrs. Lydia, have you ever thought about who God is trying to reach through you?" Ryan turned to leave, "I'll be here a 5:30AM" and he walked out.

I turned and looked at the canvas painting on the wall. I didn't notice it before but Ryan looked a lot like Grandpa Manoah. I thanked Elizabeth and said my good nights and went upstairs to my room. I was so mad at Ryan I could scream. I thought, "God why do I hate strong men? Is it me or is it them? Dad was in the military so he was gone most of my young life. It was mom and me against the world. Could it be something to do with him not being around?"

I looked at the letters. I had not opened Grandpa's so I sat down on the bed. As I opened it, I was seeing in my mind, his resemblance to Ryan. I was almost prejudice against grandpa before it was opened.

"Dear Lydia, I can't wait to see you and spend time and share. You are a thinker and it may be difficult for you to open the gate. A lot is riding on you, not only for you but millions of people will suffer beyond what I can describe to you, if you don't get the diaries. I know it is a lot to ask of you at this stage of your life but I assure you that you will be glad you did. Now, let's you and I talk about how to pray. 1 Thessalonians 5:23 says you have three compartments, body, soul and spirit. The temple of God is the same, outer court, inner court and holy of holies. You, have to get to the Holy of Holies to open the South Gate. Let me walk you through it, one step at a time.

When you first close your eyes to pray, the five senses of your body, the outer court, will be what you are most aware of. But, stay in prayer and you'll pass through the outer court.

Then, after a while, you will become aware of your heart beat and your emotions and mind, which is your soul, the inner court will come in to focus. Again, stay in prayer and don't open your eyes and you'll pass through the inner court.

Then, as your breathing slows you will approach what is known as the 'theta brain wave stage'. This is called the dream state. This is where you may enter the Holy of Holies! At this point, you will be instructed what to do. It is where you open the gate! You must follow this path in prayer because only your spirit can open the South Gate.

We'll be waiting for you. We love you and your dad sends his love. Grandpa Manoah."

By now, I'm done for. Whatever defensive mechanism I had in place has been crippled. I read it over and over and over. I wondered what he meant by, 'millions will suffer'. I knew sleep was out of the question as I laid down for the night but I set my alarm for five AM, just in case.

Chapter Five

Cohutta Mountain

I rolled over and hit the alarm. I don't remember ever sleeping so sound. So much for not sleeping. I made my way to the shower and was ready for action within a few moments. Down the steps I went as I was hearing sounds coming from the kitchen. Elizabeth and Katrina were already up and breakfast was hot and ready. Just then, I heard the front door open. It was Ryan and he had that same boyish smile on that he had yesterday morning when I met him.

"Morning ladies." he said as he went for the coffee pot. "God! This is going to be a great day." he didn't even act like he remembered or was bothered with our, slightly harsh, conversation last night. "Mrs. Lydia, are you ready for today?" he asked and every eye in the room turned toward me. "Yes sir, I am." I said with a smile. The smell of the coffee was pleasant and the heat from the stove made me and the eggs warm inside. Katrina handed me a plate and I sat down at the breakfast bar.

Ryan grabbed the chair right beside me and looked straight at me, "My family and I prayed all night for you. There isn't any way to explain to you how much we need for you to succeed. Whatever you need, know that I am on your side and if I can do anything, just say so and it'll be done." It was grateful to hear, "that mean so much. Thank You." I told him. Elizabeth came over and sat down, "Mrs. Lydia, do you have it figured out yet? I mean, do you know how to open the South Gate?" I nodded my head as I took a sip of coffee. "Grandpa's letter showed me the way, but I don't think it's going to be as simple as it sounds."

Ryan looked at his watch, "Time for us to scoot" he said just as he lifted his cup for a final drink. Both Elizabeth and Katrina gave me a hug and I followed Ryan to his truck. "Boy, you need a step ladder to get up to the handle", I said as a compliment, knowing it would boost his ego. He laughed as he opened my door from the inside, "want me to throw you a rope?" I made it up into the seat. "Well done", he said and put it in gear. It wasn't long before we were at the top of the mountain.

As I climbed down from the truck, I looked at Ryan and said, "I will never make fun of a jacked-up truck again! We would have been hours hiking up that old road bed. Those ruts were so deep, I could have sat in them and you could have drove over me without touching my head." Ryan smiled just slightly, "Ma'am, that wasn't an old road bed. That was a wash." I looked back the way we came. It was still too dark inside the forest to see if he was pulling my leg. "Come on, the clearing is just over that ridge.

Remember the full moon yesterday morning?" Ryan asked as we walked through the trees. "I will never forget it Ryan. That was the most beautiful thing I have ever saw." He continued, "Remember how you said that if we were on that mountain that you thought we could touch it?" Just then, we entered in to a clearing. There it was! Perfectly eye level! "Mrs. Lydia, I would like to introduce you to the Moon. Mr. Moon, this is Mrs. Lydia." I started to walk closer but Ryan stopped me, "rocks are loose out there and we can't see them as good in the moonlight." I was moon struck, "Ryan, oh my God, Ryan, it's laying on a blanket of snow but we're warm! Ryan, is God up here? This has got to be Heaven!" I hadn't notice but Ryan had a wool army blanket and he was laying it out on the ground. "Mrs. Lydia, I brought this for you to sit on. I didn't know how long we would be up here, so I thought you could use it." As I sat down, I said, "How very thoughtful. I take back calling you a smartass man child." "You didn't" he responded quickly. "I must have thought it. Either way, I take it back." We both laughed.

"Mrs. Lydia, do you know how to pray?" I looked out at the moon, "I thought I did until last night. I guess I'm going to learn how to today." Ryan never sat down. "I believe it will be easier for you if I get out of your way, so I'm going over into the edge of the woods. I won't take my eyes off you so you feel free to follow your spirit." Ryan walked about fifty or sixty steps away and sat down beside a huge tree.

I didn't know what to feel, I just looked out at the moon. It was so close I could see the craters. I watched as the moon light seemed to evaporate into the dawning sky. Soon the sun started melting away the night like frost melting away from a window. I heard the birds beginning to sing praises to the day, I felt the moisture rising-up from the valleys below. Just then, I realized what Grandma Margaret said in her letter, "you will be above the clouds". I looked back at the moon, the blanket of snow I thought I saw was the clouds! I was above the clouds! There I was again, the moon setting on my right side and the sun rising on my left. Only this time, I was on top of the world.

I closed my eyes and started to think about grandpa's instructions. I thought about my five senses. I took the time to feel each one. I asked myself what was important about each one. As I thought about each and what it would feel like if I didn't have it, I began to thank God for giving me eyes to see the moon and the clouds and the sun. I thanked him for my ears and all the sounds that I have heard in my life. I thanked him for my nose as I could smell the forest around me. Then I thanked him for the ability to feel the warmth coming from the blanket and finally I thanked him for my sense of taste as I thought what life would be like if I didn't have it.

As I started to taste, I realized the sound of my heart and I knew by grandpa's letter that I was moving into the inner court. With my eyes still closed, I tried to look around the darkness inside and imagine it was like a room with the light turned off. I imagined myself feeling around for a light switch.

All of the sudden, I heard myself singing. I was singing on the inside. I was still aware of my body and my mouth was closed. I could hear breath coming in and going out. I could hear my heart beat and yet, I was singing. "Jesus loves me this I know, for the Bible tells me so. Little ones to him belong, we are weak but he is strong. . ." Then it happened! Everything was light. I was standing at the edge of a field. In the field was a baby in diapers and a large angry bull with long horns. I looked up and there was a Christmas gift floating down from the sky with a beautiful red ribbon and it came to rest between the baby and the bull. The bull was determined to open the gift. He kicked it, he snorted and charged the gift, picking it up by his horns and throwing it in the sky and dropping it back to the ground. No matter how mean and determined the bull was, he could not open the gift.

Finally, the bull walked away and the baby crawled up beside the gift and with just one small hand, pulled on the ribbon and the bow untied, and the box fell open. Inside the box was a key. Then I heard a voice, "Unless you become like a little child, you will in no wise enter in." The picture was gone and my eyes opened to see miles and miles of valleys and hills.

The clouds had lifted to reveal the treasures of the valleys below. It took a minute for my senses to return. I heard something to my right, it was Ryan. "Are you okay? I saw you jerk like you were hit with something. I thought a tree limb or something might have hit you." I looked up at him. I must have had a dazed look. "Mrs. Lydia, Are you with me?" Ryan said as he grabbed me by both arms. "I am with you, give me a minute", as I must have smiled a mile wide because I saw him smiling back at me almost as big. It took me a good while to regain myself.

Ryan was exuberant, like the first night, or morning I met him. "Mrs. Lydia, I have seen lots of people get caught up in the spirit in church but this is the first time I have ever seen God call someone up in the woods. I think I could back flip off this mountain! Can you tell me about it? Please!?" I looked at Ryan, "What day is it?" He was still smiling, "It is Tuesday, December 22, 2010 at 12:22 in the afternoon.

We are on top of Cohutta Mountain and the Lord just spoke to you and if you don't tell me, I'm going to bust!" I realized what he just said, I looked at him, "I think He just gave me the key to the Gate! We need to get back to the house." I think he picked me up with one arm and the blanket with the other and in no more than one or two steps, I was buckled up in his truck. The next thing I remember we were bouncing off the mountain trail, on to a paved road.

Back Home

Kevin, Katrina and Elizabeth were waiting on the front porch. As Ryan pulled up to the door, Kevin opened my door and took me out. I asked, "How did you know we were coming?" Elizabeth held up her hand to show her phone, "cell phones." Kevin never let my feet touch the ground and I was on the couch in the great room before I could say a word.

"Okay, Okay, I'm alright. Slow down just a minute, I'm fine." I just kept trying to calm them down. After a few more minutes, I realized they were the calm ones and it was me that wasn't completely zoned in. I looked at Ryan, "Can you explain this to me?" He was still grinning, "Mrs. Lydia, God has spoken to you! And if you don't tell us what He said, we ain't ever leaving here." I realized I was slumped down, sitting half sideways on the couch so I sat myself up.

I told them the whole story, from start to finish. All four of them were smiling with tears rolling down their cheeks. Kevin said, "I never really knew how to pray. I think I do now." Katrina joined in, "I think I have gotten to the inner court a time or two but wow!" Ryan had never sat down, he had so much energy that he couldn't sit still. "God has spoken to me many times, but I have never had it explained is such a perfect way before. I think I could teach that at Sunday school." Elizabeth appeared star struck. I looked at her to see what her thoughts were.

"You have the key Mrs. Lydia, and you are at South Gate. Now what?" The room seemed to sober suddenly. My mind raced through everything I had been told and everything I had read, "Grandma's letter said she would be waiting for me in the greenhouse when I returned!" We all jumped up and headed for the deck. We made it to the bottom deck and Ryan stopped us all, "She has to go alone." Somehow, I knew he was right but I so wanted us all to go rushing in. I had this feeling or maybe a need for someone besides me to see Grandma Margaret with their own eyes.

I stared at the greenhouse, then looked at each of them. I stepped down the three steps on to the walkway and counted my steps as I walked. I didn't know why I counted, maybe out of a nervous reaction, but it was ninety-one steps to the door. I remembered both Grandma Fayth and Ryan mentioning the ninety-one years. I thought, "There is no way that was not planned." I reached to open the door, it was locked! I tried it again but still, nothing. I took a step back, I looked back at Ryan and them.

I turned back toward the door and closed my eyes to pray. I didn't have to go through the outer court, I was instantly in the dark inner court. Again, I looked and felt around for a light switch. I knew the box with the key was somewhere in this inner court. There appeared a light in the upper right-hand corner and I started to reach for it and as I did, I noticed the key was in my hand. My mind seemed to ponder why or how I had the key and without noticing, the greenhouse door was in front of the key.

I placed the key into the lock and turned. I heard it click and my eyes opened. I was still in front of the green house, I looked, once again, at the crew. I stepped forward and grabbed the handle and turned, it opened! I slowly walked in, almost expecting a ghost to jump out from behind the door, even though it was a glass door and I could see everything. The door closed behind me and I scanned the greenhouse to the right and then to the left. Somebody was there! Down the second isle, about halfway down, working on a plant of some kind. I moved into the aisle so I could get a clear look. I couldn't see if it was a man or a woman, but they had on a brown over coat and bending down working on plants. I stepped closer, "Grandma?"

My heart pounding so loud I knew the person could hear it if I stepped any closer. She stood up and I saw the scarf over her head that was in the portrait. She looked at me and smiled. My legs began to get weak and the world was starting to spin. "Lydia! You don't have time for that. Come over here. I have to show you something.", and she turned back to the plant work.

Her voice was kind but strong, it stunned me back in control. "Yes Ma'am.", I said and I walked closer. She stood up and reach out and hugged me, "I won't break girl." she said with a more, gentle voice. I hugged her and stepped back to look in to her face. "Grandma Margaret?" She grinned and laughed, "After all you have went through to get here and you think God would send you a substitute teacher!" We both laughed. "Where is Grandpa?" "He gets the evenings and nights and I get the day time. Since you spent half the day on the mountain, we have to cover a lot in a short while to get in what you have to learn today."

She pointed at a plant, "Do you know what that is?" I looked, "No Ma'am." She picked a piece and held it up for me to see, "Barley Grass. Barley grass is one of the best foods on the planet and it contains eight essential amino acids. In fact, eating whole-grain barley will regulate blood sugar for about 10 hours. Also, it is very high in organic sodium, which dissolves calcium deposited on the joints and, also replenishes the sodium in the lining of your stomach. This fixes digestion by improving the production of hydrochloric acid in the stomach. It also has thirty times more vitamin B1 and eleven times the amount of calcium than there is in cow's milk. It has almost five times the iron content of spinach and close to seven times the vitamin C of oranges. Technically, it could sustain people from the cradle to the grave. The health benefits include relief from ulcerative colitis, prevention and treatment of cancer, strengthening of immune system, cleansing and detoxification of the body, protection from radiation and cellular damage, ability to fight addiction and regenerate damaged cells and tissues. It maintains healthy skin, acid-alkali balance, contributes in the bone metabolism, promotes agility and exerts rejuvenating effects on the entire body. And I love these heads roasted!"

I stood there completely speechless, she was a walking encyclopedia. "Wow grandma. You are amazing!" She gave me a stern teacher type look, "Hold on a minute child. I am not here to impress you. I am here to impress upon you, the things you have to know to save millions. You don't think God would go to all this trouble just to impress you, do you?"

The seriousness of the pass few days seemed to all come into view with that one statement. For the first time, I realized that not only was this not about me but that something very big and bad must be coming, in the near future. "I'm sorry grandma. I'll pay close attention." Her face softened a little but you could tell she was a woman on a mission. "Lydia, do you know the difference between perennial plants and annual plants?" "Oh yes. Annuals grow one year and die out but perennials grow continually, year after year." She started walking toward another plant, "Very good. Now can you tell me what

93

percentage of plants on the planet are perennial compared to annual?" I shook my head no. "Ninety five percent are perennial. Now, please explain to me why America's and most of the world's food sources are annual?" I wasn't sure what to say and she apparently noticed it.

"Lydia, you are an actuary, you worked for the census bureau and now the congressional budget office. You know more demographics about the American population than any American President in history and seeing the big picture will help you to retain memory.

Now, how many people are there on the planet?" Okay, now we're talking. I know this, "just over 6 billion." She moved further down the aisle, "correct. Now, if you divided up the usable land, just in the United States, how much land would each person have?" I had to do my math on that one, "There is 3.79 million square miles of usable land. There are 640 acres per square mile. So, I figure right at 7 acres per adult and child.

Meaning that a man, wife and two children could own about 28 acres." This time she smiled, "You really are good, but to be exact, 7.77 acres per person. The purpose of this exercise is two-fold, first an observation of governance.

Humans are the only creature on this planet that have to pay to live here. Do you think that was God's Plan? No, it was not! If a group of like-minded people came together, bought every newborn an acre of land and then gave it a fruit tree, nut tree or fruit bearing perennial for each of its birthdays. By the time it turned 18 years old, what else would it need? The excuse for abortion and wars is over population. Is that really the case when the fact is that every man, woman and child on the planet can stand in Texas and each have 1500 square feet?

This greenhouse is only 3000 square feet and there are two of us in it, and I assure you there is more than enough food for us to live your entire life. Second point is fear. Fear is promoted, in order to navigate the people for control and profit.

You will learn over the next few days that fear is the absolute opposite of faith. The two main instruments used to create fear are the food source and health. That answers the original query, 'Why America's and most of the world's food sources are annual?'

Commerce over Conscience. The Bible is replete with the destructive patterns of commerce over conscience, but Manoah will be teaching you about that." Again, I stood speechless and it appeared she was not going to look up from working the next set of plants until I responded. I tried to get my brain around the, 'why I was here' question.

"Grandma, why me and why now? Why am I supposed to learn all this and what is going to happen that could cause millions to die?" She stood up and picked a twig off a tree in the center aisle, "before I answer that, do you know what this tree is?" I shook my head again. "Moringa. In Africa it is called, 'Nebedaye', which means, 'Never Die'. I could spend an hour telling you about this one, but I'm leaving that for your homework. I will just say this, it cures over 300 diseases."

She pointed toward the bench seat at the end of the row. We sat down and she took my hands, "Lydia, Manoah will teach you about your times and how to read the round calendar, what church folks nowadays call prophecy. The Bible says there is no hidden interpretation of scripture and that God is not a respecter of person. That means, what He showed to Daniel, Isaiah, Ezekiel and all the prophets, He will show to you. Child, it is not, 'what could cause millions to die', but what will cause millions to die? It is not one thing but many things all happening in this one life cycle.

Let's start with a basic value chart. What is life? What is it at its base?" She looked at me in such a way that I knew I was supposed to answer. " Health and food, I guess would be the essentials." She smiled and added, "and shelter. Food, clothing, and shelter should produce health. Those are the most basic values.

Now, are they taught in K through 12? I'll answer it for you, NO! Do you rent or have a mortgage? I know that answer too, mortgage. You mean to tell me that in thirty years you couldn't build or secure your home? You couldn't faith in a home? You have been raised in Egypt and Babylon. When you borrow, you are borrowing from your future.

Credit is spending your tomorrows.

The word Egypt means captivity and Babylon means confusion. You have been raised by a world system that is designed to keep you bound and in captivity. Our job is to set you free and to allow you to manifest who you are.

Just in the United States since its founding, there have been two depressions, 1837 and 1929. Solomon said that there is no new thing in the earth. What was, will be, but men forget. For everything there is a time and a season or cycle.

These are the patterns of prophecy that Manoah will teach you about. And another depression is very, very near. Manoah will also show you how to establish times. In scripture, times are events and seasons are cycles. You must learn to trust in God. Your name is Lydia Fayth, which means, 'Trust and

96

Faith'. They are two separate words with two complete separate functions.

Faith is offence and Trust is defense.

One is moving forward and the other is standing your ground. Imagine faith as pushing something and trust is the foundation you are standing on. Knowing God and knowing his ways and patterns is where your ability to trust comes from. Jesus said, 'no sign shall be given except that of Jonah', He was speaking of a pattern of God that He bet His life on. Faith is the substance of things hoped for, it is you pushing. I just don't want you to be operating in faith and standing on skates."

She stood up, so I did the same. We started walking down the outside row of plants as she continued. "Manoah taught you about the trichotomy. The body, soul and spirit. Let's deal with that for a moment. You need to feed all three, you need to discipline and teach all three and you may need to heal one of the three at different times. Some people need healed in all three, some just in the body and some in the soul, but almost all need healing in the spirit.

I am teaching you about God's food source and medicines. That educates the soul, but what I am really doing is changing your value system which is educating the spirit. Do you see?" "Kinda", I responded.

She picked another plant but continued, "Let me show you values in two other examples. Have you ever seen a news report about a thief?" "Yes Ma'am." "But you don't steal, why?" "It hurts even to think about the question!" I said. "That is because from an early age you were taught, 'Thou shall not steal.' but the thief was not taught it. You have the value, he does not.

Have you ever seen a mother give a toy to a child and when the child finishes playing with the toy, she does not require the child to put up the toy?" I nodded. "Now watch this closely, everything in life has a response tied to it. If you get a car, there is a set of responses. If you go to school, there is a set of responses. If you go to work, there is a set of responses. If you get a boyfriend or husband, there are a lot of responses. And even though the mother is responding in what she understands is love, she has handicapped the child and somewhere around age twelve to fourteen, they will buy the child a pet and say, 'this will teach them responsibility'.

Responsibility is a moving toward value and Neglect is a spirit to move away from. Unknown to her, she has opened the door to the Spirit of Neglect. A strongman that will haunt the life of that child for years and years. The Spirit of Neglect will cause you to neglect your health, neglect your finances, neglect to make the call and even neglect your husband or children.

Response is a value and it is a great servant but a very poor master. Time is a great servant and a gruel master. Money is a great servant but the worst of slave masters. Each of these are to be your servants. Each of these are values that must be placed into the spirit. Your soul, which is your mind and emotions that control the will to act, may be educated with the intricacies of each discipline and you never act upon that education. I am sure you have met people who know what to do but never do it." "Yes Ma'am. I sure have, and a lot of them."

"One more before I go." she held up another plant, "You know?" By now we both shook our heads, no. "Queen Ann's Lace. Smell of it." She held it up for me to smell. "Hum, smells
98

like a carrot" I replied. She grinned really big, "that's because it is! Wild carrot is what it's called. See that little black dot in the center of the flower?" I nodded. "That is a must see! If there is no dot, it is poisonous, there are a lot of look-a-likes. There is one that looks like it but doesn't have the dot, it will kill a 2000, pound cow. So, whatever you do, see the dot! But this plant is, considered to be a weed. You almost can't kill it. It grows alongside of almost every road in the country. Learn what it looks like, memorize it and incorporate it into your pot roast and your turkey dinners.

Now, I have to go and you need to rest before Manoah arrives." She leaned close and hugged. I didn't want her to go. Somehow, deep inside, I felt like I was losing her. "Do you have to leave? When do I get to see you again?" She held me by my shoulders and looked me in the eyes, "Tomorrow morning. As early as you would like. I'll be right here." I smiled but was fighting back tears.

She turned and walked down the row. When she reached the end, she turned right and passed behind a tall shrub. She didn't appear on the other side. I stood there, looking in every direction, scanning the greenhouse. I noticed hundreds of plants, I looked at the three plants she gave me then back at the greenhouse, I thought, "tomorrow will be a long day". That made me happy inside.

The Evening

Back inside, everyone was waiting as I walked over and sat down. It seemed like they were afraid to ask and I felt almost afraid to say. Finally, I broke the silence, "It is all true.

She was there." Elizabeth covered her mouth with both hands as if to muffle her scream. You could see her eyes sparkling through the swell of tears. Katrina grabbed Elizabeth with a hug, while Kevin looked at Ryan and said, "I knew it was true. I just knew it!" Ryan was up walking back and forth, "I feel like running through town pointing my finger at everyone I see and say, 'I told you so, I told you so, I told you so!"

I continued to share the entire event with them and told them I had to rest for Grandpa's visit. Elizabeth asked if I could eat something, I declined and headed up stairs to rest. As I laid down across the bed, I closed my eyes and instantly found myself praying. I thought how I probably would never again be able to close my eyes without knowing I was entering the inner court.

I don't know how long I slept but when I opened my eyes, the room was dusky dark. I got up and turned on the light, scanning the room for grandpa. Slightly disappointed, I headed down stairs and walked out the front door and looked at the driveway fountain. The brisk December air reminded me of the snow-covered streets of Washington DC and my drive here. I walked around the fountain and decided to grab a jacket before going down to the greenhouse, thinking that somehow it may be the meeting place.

As I headed back toward the front door, I noticed someone standing on the shadowy moonlight balcony. I stopped, knowing I wanted it to be grandpa. He spoke, "Lydia Fayth, you look just like your mother when she was your age. Care to join me for an evening chat?"

It was him! Grandpa Manoah Elbertson. I dashed through the doors and up the stairs and slowed down just in time as he was opening the balcony door for me.

"Slow down child. Life's too short to run through it." I stood there looking up at him. He was well over six feet, neatly bearded but clean and crisp. He had a farm demeanor about his clothing but at the same time he would not have been out of place in a bank or law office. His clothing kind of took second place to his strong but friendly facial characteristics. I couldn't help myself, I latched on to him with a hug. It felt like all my strength was coming from him. Some kind of deep, heritage, sort of like hugging your father returning from a war after being gone for many years. It was like the you, in you, returning.

He looked at me and began, "Young lady, we have a lot to cover and I will probably unload more on you than your wagon can carry so, do you have a notebook and pen?" I said yes and went to my nightstand. I noticed he did not come in the room. "You can come in." I said but he just stood there. As I came back out on to the balcony, he responded,

"Young lady, in my day, fathers did not go into daughter's rooms after they reached age twelve. A man has no business in a girl's room." I looked at him while he spoke, he was serious. "Yes Sir. I'm sorry." I replied. "For what? You haven't done anything wrong. Your response indicates that you are around people who place blame. I did not blame you of any wrong doing. I was giving you a statement of my belief.", he said as he turned to take a seat in one of two, rather large vine woven rockers.

He continued, "First, let's cover your questions. What ya got for me?" I thought about how I asked grandma, so I just asked it the same way, "Why me and why now?" He was slightly rocking as he began, "Do you have more than one

dress?" I was caught off guard by the question, "Yes Sir."
"What would you say to a dress if it asked you, 'Why me?'" he smiled. "That is the simplest and most direct answer. God chose you. He made you and does not need your permission to use you. But if you want the long version I have to ask you a question first.

" I smiled and said, "Ask away because I really want the long version." He quit rocking and leaned forward, "Are you asking for self-edification or are you asking to understand God's purpose?"

I thought on both questions, "I think both. I really want to know the purpose I was chose but at the same time I don't know if I'm qualified for the purpose."

He leaned back and slowly started rocking, "Fair enough. Let's correct your locus. You answered both questions with, 'I' and used, 'I' five times in two sentences. 'I think, I really, I was chosen, I don't and I'm qualified.' We are not going to be able to build a future on an 'I'. God chose Abram and spoke to him about his children four generations in the future and how they would need to be freed. They would be enslaved to a foreign country because of the sins of the Amorites. The method of enslavement was accomplished because they did not control their own food source. Note, that it was the fourth generation that fell and four generations before Moses. Abraham, Isaac, Jacob and Joseph. Joseph was sold into slavery by his own brothers. Just like America is being sold into slavery by its own leaders. You cannot set a minimum wage in America then have free trade agreements with countries with lesser wages. All product producing jobs leave your country. This can only happen by two types of politicians, very, very stupid ones or revenuers, and most likely they are one in the same.

They're reasoning is based on projected tax revenue from imports but totally ignore revenue lost by job losses. All revenue is not created equal.

You are the fourth generation departed from an agricultural base. Your generation does not know how to grow, process or store food. Your generation is being sold as commerce over conscience. The fourth generation that does not own their own food source.

The Angel told me and Margaret that this would become possible because the sins of the Darwinites. It is the 'Me God' versus 'We God', the self-serving verses the brotherhood of man and the magnitude of your generation will alter life on this planet for the next 2160 years. You, Mrs. Lydia Fayth are in the center of the hour glass. Your generation is the bottle's neck and your generation alone will determine outcomes that will direct the course of events and shape life for generations to come.

Now, you tell me, Why you and Why now?" I think my mouth had dropped open at some point because I consciously closed it. I sat back in the rocker and started rocking slowly, processing the information. I was trying to form a time matrix in my head so I could place each thought in a binary position. I just knew there had to be a circular theory argument in play but without more confirmed factual data, it was going to be hard to accurately examine and separate hard, fact from theology.

Grandpa must have read my mind, he smiled and chuckled softly, "I love a good thinker. You are right now, evaluating possibilities and percentages of likelihoods. Let me guess, you are trying to establish a scale with binary reasoning.

God calls that the, tree of knowledge of good and evil. All can comprehend good by comparison to evil, beauty defines ugly, high defines low, short defines long and all definitions and comprehensions are based on a comparison.

My child, the fallacy that can occur comes by not having the correct information to compare with. I am sure that in life and business, you have made good decisions that turned out poorly. This would be because you did not have all the facts when you made the decision. Later, when all the facts were made know, you had a different conclusion.

Let me help you a little. If you had to rank the top five nations on the planet in any category, where would America place?" That was a no brainer, "First". He lost his smile, "You really think so?" I said, "Absolutely". He shook his head in disbelief, "

Let me say, I love America but for your generation to properly navigate the church, you must realize there is a problem and then identify the variables of the problems. Of the people reaching the age 65 in America, 54 out of every hundred are dead. America does not lead the world in longevity, in fact, America is 49th in life expectancy. Now, 36 of every hundred are totally dependent for food or health or both. 54 plus 36 equals 90% of the people reaching age 65 in America are dead broke or dead. That sounds like to me that you are only winning 10% of the time. Is that the way you want your future to look? How about your children's future? When you have children, do you want them to have a 90% chance of failing? How about for anyone else's children?

There is only one income question I pose to illustrate why this occurs. If you get sick for a month or go on vacation for a month, do you have any income coming in?" I thought for a moment, "I could manage for a couple of months on savings but I wouldn't have any income."

He continued, "That means you have spent your entire financial life building temporary or annual incomes and have not built any perennial incomes. Your financial garden is planted with annuals. Lydia, you study economics, you know that success is like perfume, the more your neighbors get, the better the neighborhood gets. You can't put it on your friend and not get some on you. Just like you at work, by helping your managers be successful, makes your department successful and by doing so, makes you successful. That is, unless you have developed a, me only, style of managing. America has fallen prey to the 'Me First, Me God'.

It will be hard for you to establish binary reasoning between personal and social values to financial outcomes because it will always feel like a circular argument. When I establish facts in one field of study, then apply it to another area of study, it will be difficult to scale. But the bottom line is that wisdom has looked at your financial garden, evaluated probable outcomes and without change, your destination will be in the ninety percent bucket.

So, if you will allow me, we do not have time to concrete each thought singularly. What I will promise you is that I will not use presuppositions of factual, information to establish foundations for theology. So, for the next two days and three evenings, you will have to allow us to make our case and then, with all the information your binary reasoning will establish a firm resolve."

I wanted to believe him and if I were to be honest with

myself, I did, but I think my analytic mind kicks in like a parachute at any sign of insecurity. And what I was hearing was by no means giving me a feeling of strength. "Okay Grandpa, can you explain to me what, when, where, why and how is this going to happen? Grandma said there is no hidden interpretation of scripture so you would be able to explain to me how you arrive at your conclusions."

He must have noticed that I was getting cold as darkness fell, "Here. Take my coat and I will be glad to help you understand." I wrapped his coat around my shoulders and sat back down. He started to pace a short distance in front of our rockers, "First let us go over what you have learned today about prayer.

You learned the path to the secret place, the Holy of Holies. I would like you to notice something very important that you may not have realized. The keys that opened each door. Psalms 100 verse 4 says, 'Enter into his gates with thanksgiving, and into his courts with praise: be thankful unto him, and bless his name'. Did you notice that you thanked Him for the value of your five senses as you imagined life without them? And did you notice that you began to sing praises in the inner court?"

I was recalling my morning prayer on the mountain, as he was talking, "Your right, I was!" He smiled and stopped pacing for a moment, "I developed a habit in my night time prayer, when I was young, that I would ask you to try to develop. Before your bedtime prayer, imagine, for a moment, that when you woke the following morning, that you only have what you thanked Him for the night before. What would you have today if it was only what you thanked Him for last night?

Did you thank Him for your health? How about your mother? Or your husband Robert? Your job, your country, your freedoms? How about thanking Him for your future? This is the first key to the throne room of God."

I smiled somewhat hoping to cover my thoughts as the sense of guilt and loss filled my mind. "Grandpa, that is a habit I would like to have."

He returned to his rocker and began, "First we must raise you up so your eyes can be opened. Revelations 4:1 John says, 'After this I looked, and, behold, a door was opened in heaven: and the first voice which I heard was as a trumpet talking with me; which said, Come up hither, and I will shew thee things which must be hereafter.' Notice the term, 'come up hither'?" I nodded, "Yes Sir."

He continued, "Perception is a peculiar concept. It is defined as, the organization, identification, and interpretation of information in order to understand your environment. Now, would you say that a pilot's perception of the ocean differs from that of a pirate?" Again, I nodded. "How about a turtle's perception compared to a giraffe's? For the turtle to see from the giraffe's, he would have to be raised up. So, to perceive the things of God, it would be natural that you must look at it from God's perspective. Well let's get you to, 'come up hither'.

Follow along with this illustration, if a young man was driving his motorcycle 50 miles per hour at night. He would have to see 100 yards in front of him to avoid danger. If he were driving a car, 100 miles per hour at night, he would have to be able to see a quarter mile ahead to avoid danger. If he were to get on a plane doing 300 miles per hour, the pilot would have to see three miles ahead to avoid danger.

Now, let us apply that to life. You will not be able to travel any faster in life than your ability to see ahead, or should I say, your ability to navigate obstacles and dangers.

Your generation is traveling at the speed of light and you cannot see what is directly in front of you. You have the answer to any question at the tips of your fingers and by computer you can see around the world but you are totally blind. The church has made a mockery of wisdom and she has retired to her mountain.

Can you see dangerous or significant events for the next year? How about the events of the next five or ten years? Can you tell me about the five plagues? When is their beginning and when is their end? Can you tell me the day and the hour judgment comes to the White House? Can you tell me the day and the hour the famine begins? Can you tell me its seasons? Can you tell me it's summer or winter? Tell me the story of the ten virgins if you know the wisdom thereof. Do you understand the ages and stages of man? Have you seen the four horses descending upon the earth in your generation? Can you tell me the names of their riders? Can you show me the wheel inside of a wheel? Tell me, if you know, the meaning of the number 666, show me the matrix thereof. In Psalms 90 verse 12 the people of God prayed, 'Teach us to number our days, that we may apply our hearts unto wisdom.' and God did. If you do not value this knowledge, then do not seek it for those that hunger and thirst after righteousness shall be filled.

Lydia, God has opened a door for you, and I am here to invite you to come up. In Numbers 12 verse 6, God said He would speak to you in dreams. When you pray before you retire for the evening, ask God any question that you will. He told

Jeremiah, 'Call unto me and I will answer thee and show thee wonderful and mighty things thou knowest not.' And Jesus said, 'Ask and ye shall receive.' Now, it is time for me to go. May I ask you to return to your room?"

At that, he stood up. He had an official type air that didn't seem to require a response. "Yes Sir", I said as I handed him his coat. I turned and walked into the room, turned on the lamp beside the bed. I returned to close the balcony door and he was nowhere to be seen. I looked at the clock, 12:31AM. I knew that the time would be important to remember so I wrote it down. I started jotting down everything he said and made another section for grandma. By 1:30 I had gathered my request and laid down and began to pray.

The First Dream

"Lord, I want to thank you for everything you have brought me to and in the days to come I will be preparing a list of many things and people I am thankful for and I will be mindful of them every night. Today, I have learned a great deal but I need to be able to rightfully divide facts from fiction in order to make good and meaningful decisions. Will you show me how to separate the good from the bad? Amen" At that, she turned out the light and went to bed.

My eyes opened, I looked around. Where was I? I was on a stage, a church stage. The room was full of people and they were all looking at me. I was there but at the same time, I was staring at myself from somewhere above my right shoulder.

There was my body, I could hear it speaking but I could feel the emotion of being embarrassed. I had never spoke in front of a church before. It felt very strange. I watched and listened. I had in my right hand a pitcher of crystal clear water. In my left hand, I had a handful of dirt. I was pouring the dirt into the clean water. At that moment, instantly I was back in my room. It was daylight and I was standing at the balcony door. I looked in the bed and my body was there asleep. I walked closer to look. It was me. I felt an extreme sense of joy. I thought, "The God that created the Heavens and Earth, has just answered my question!" I looked toward the ceiling but it was not there. I stared into the heaven and thought about the pitcher and the dirt. How clearly, I could see putting something dirty into something clean. As I was thanking Him for the answer, I realized that the information still did not allow me to distinguish fact from fiction. I began to feel sadness and looked back to the bed. I closed my eyes and asked God if I had miss understood. When I opened my eyes, I was again on the church stage. This time I had a pitcher of clean water in my right hand and a pitcher of dirty water in my left. As I looked out to the crowd, they all had empty glasses. I was asking them which water they would prefer to drink. Once again, I felt a sense of joy because the answer would be obvious. It was like a blink, one moment I was in church, the next I am walking in the garden near the greenhouse. I looked around, even thou everything was growing like the beginning of spring, it felt like I was the only person on the planet. I sat down on a garden bench. I thought about what I had seen in the church vision. I realized that if a person could see the difference between what was good or clean and what was dirty or bad, they would naturally choose clean. I told God, "If they can see what is clean, they will always choose it." There seemed to be no barrier between us, I heard in my mind, or maybe it was my spirit, "People smoke and drink and both clearly cause harm?" This caused me to rethink the purpose of the vision. What was I missing? I started feeling as if God was speaking but for some unknown reason, I was not able to understand. I started feeling as if He had chosen the wrong person. I spoke toward the ground, "God I'm sorry. You are speaking and I thank you but I still cannot see how to discern that which is good and truth. After a few minutes, I looked up and about twenty steps away was a pitcher of clean, clear water sitting on the edge of a slightly raised bed. I stood up and walked over. Without thinking, I picked up the pitcher, held it up to the sky and stared through it. The sunlight seemed to fill the water, like energy to a battery. I looked down at the garden. There was a small tomato plant inside the raised bed and just on the outside of the bed was a small bunch of vine type weeds. I realized, as I stood there holding the water above the plants, it was my choice which I watered, that which would grow up and give me fruit, life and health or that which would drag me down, bear nothing and destroy that which was good.

The vision was clear to me now. The three lessons were the trichotomy of man, body, soul and spirit. Many people decide what is right or wrong by what their body wants. Others decide with their mind or emotions. But a person of the spirit can discern truth by evaluating outcomes. Even thou my work is a constant calculation of facts and data, truth and fact in most cases, are not co-habitable.

Chapter Six

Day Two

I rolled over in the bed, the sun already was filling my room. I jumped up and ran to the balcony door. I looked down at the greenhouse and thought about grandma. As I turned back toward the bed, 'de-ja-vu'. I stared at the bed just as I expected to see my body lying in it.

The entire dream came rushing in. There was a weakness in my legs but a joy in my heart all at the same time. I knelt, down beside the bed and placed my head in the sheets. "My God, my God, you have spoken to me! Everything I have known to be important is pouring out of me. Your value is greater than my mind can hold. Teach me thy ways oh Lord! Teach me thy ways!"

It took me a while to regain myself. I dashed for the shower, got dressed, darted down the step and out the door. I couldn't wait to see grandma. I opened the greenhouse door, almost knowingly, looking for her in the aisles. There she was, sitting on the bench across from the entrance. She smiled as I came over to sit down.

"Good morning. I hope you slept well." she turned slightly toward me as I sat down. "I slept out of this world! God answered a direct question for me! Grandpa taught me how to ask and it worked! It really worked!" She was excited for me, "Oh Lydia, that is the greatest news I could hear. What a breakthrough."

I proceeded to unload the entire vision on her and what it

meant to me. She took special note about when people could clearly see what was clean and healthy that God said many still do not chose what is best.

Grandma stood up and reached for my hand to bring me along, "Let's walk and study for a while. God has demonstrated an important fact about the nature of people. Do you remember us discussing the trichotomy?" I nodded. "Let's look at that a little closer. I want to give you a visual understanding of sickness, disease and the infected spirit."

She broke off a small branch from a shrub and started drawing on the dirt floor. She drew three circles, one inside another until we had a drawing of a three-ringed target. "She said, "The outer ring is your body, the next ring is your soul and the inner ring is the spirit. Now, when the body gets damaged or cut, it bleeds blood and if not cared for, it will get infected. Correct?" Again, I nodded.

"The next ring is your soul, which is the mind, emotions and your will to act. This is the area of 'dis-ease'. Have you ever had your emotions hurt? Has anyone ever said something that hurt you?" I was shaking my head, "Oh yeah!" She continued, "the Bible says, 'The words of a talebearer are as wounds, and they go down into the innermost parts of the belly.' It actually says it twice.

So, when the mind and emotions get cut, what does it bleed?" I paused to process the question. I stared at her drawing and said, "Spirit?" She had drawn a line through the two outer rings, "Correct. Now, can you explain to me, spirit?" I stared at the drawing. I was at a loss as how to say it in a picture form. "Not really", I said. She smiled a little, "Well, let me see how I can do.

First, God identifies himself, by name, out of a burning bush. Do you know what He said?" I responded, "I know that is the story of Moses." She continued, "He said to Moses, 'I AM THAT I AM: and he said, Thus, shalt thou say unto the children of Israel, I AM hath sent me unto you.'

That is the spirit God has placed in man, 'I AM'. You get up in the morning and say, 'I AM tired', or 'I AM excited' and if you have a bad day you might say, 'I AM fat up with bad attitudes'. You have probably said things like, 'I AM not going to shop there anymore' or 'I AM going to this place or that place.' The I AM, is your spirit. When the soul gets wounded, it bleeds the I AM, or we could say, it erodes the way you feel or think about you.

This, is why Jesus said that calling a brother a fool was killing his spirit. I can also say when God deals with a person, He always changes their I AM. The way they view themselves. Often, he changes their name, which in Bible times was a really big thing since their names had meaning in life as to what they were to accomplish. It was their character and nature, so when He changed their name, He changed their character and nature and ultimately, their destiny."

I got it! I could visually see all three parts. "Grandma, that is fantastic. I can see that." She pointed out the window of the greenhouse, "I was standing, right out there, one frosty morning and I saw a snake in the walkway and it was almost froze to death. I stopped and stared at it for a moment and God spoke to me in a vision. I saw me picking up the snake and carrying it in the greenhouse and placing it by the heat. I sat in a chair beside it until it became fully warm. It crawled over to me and bit me on the leg. I was angry and demanded, 'Why did you bite me? I was good to you!', he replied, 'You knew my nature before you got involved with me.' Then the vision was gone.

Now, young lady, can you explain the vision?" I looked back down at the three circles. I thought about the snake's nature as spirit. I looked back up at grandma, "Other than we should look for the spirit first, I don't see the whole picture."

"Lydia, the first illustration demonstrates the spirit of you. The snake illustration demonstrates the spirit of others. There will be a lot of people you meet that will need help but you need to develop your ability to discern the spirit or nature before you help. Most people you help will turn on you, and do you harm. Haven't you had boyfriends you should have discerned their spirit earlier? You should have known their nature before you took them in." She smiled as she saw my facial expression. "You bet I have! I should have let them stay outside and freeze!"

We both laughed but she continued, "This will be one of your most important skills and you will need to work on it constantly. Your spirit eye must remain open at all times. Manoah will teach you about your spirit ears before his time is up.

You have not been called to help everyone. You have been chosen to teach teachers and leaders, to be a 'Faith Coach'. To equip them to walk through the darkness that is just ahead. God has brought you here to change your, 'I AM', your spirit. The way you view you and your destiny will be changed. You will be putting off the old person and putting on a new. Just as Jacob became Israel, God will equip you for the purpose you are designed for."

I thought about my career and then about Robert. My mind quickly thought about mom. "Does this mean my career is over? I mean, do I drop everything and start over? I don't know if I am ready or even able to do that."

"No child, it doesn't mean that at all. In fact, God doesn't want you to change your career. He is going to change your spirit. He is going to turn your light on and those in need will be drawn to the light. The rest of the world will also see the light but be on guard, keep your spirit eye open, many will try to steal your light, many will be jealous and try to kill the light. The knowledge you will have will shine so bright that many will turn away from you because, in their mind, they will compare what you will be saying to their lives and they will feel your words are putting them down. The good news you bring will be like a mirror, you give them a mirror and they see dirty spots in their life. It is not the mirrors job to clean off the spots, neither is it your job. It is theirs.

Did granddad teach you about annual verses perennial incomes?" I nodded, "yes." "Was that a mirror to you?" I was still nodding, "Yes ma'am. By reflection I am able to see the two outcomes and choose the better one." She continued, "Before the information, you could not see the blemish. By your answer it is obvious that correcting this is not the mirrors job or is it granddad's. It is yours but some people will take that same mirror and scream, 'That's not fair.' and others will see you as an elitist and condemning. Then there is a whole crowd out there that will cry, 'Poor me. Can't you help me? Why won't you help me?'

You must remember, it is not your job to be their savior. That is why Jesus asked the man at the pool of Bethesda, 'Wilt thou be made whole?' In other words, is it your will to be made whole? You see child, lots of folk like being the victim. They get attention that way. Let them freeze or you'll be carrying them for the rest of your life and even then, they will blame you for their failures and lack when all you are trying to do is help prepare them to reveal the glory of God.

Lydia, time is short. If you had under 10 years to get ready for major homeland attacks and just a few months after that before the collapse of currencies, could you be ready?" I was stunned. I just stared at her. She stared back, it wasn't a trick question. I could tell, she was absolutely, serious.

I swallowed hard and suddenly the reality and meaning of my entire life stared back at me. "Grandma, can you stop the world from spinning for a day or two for me to think about this?

I got a letter from you seven days ago about an angel speaking, about an angel spinning and about an angel being prepared to speak for God. You weren't just telling a story, were you?" She shook her head no. "Well, I would like this tornado to stop for a while because I am seeing all sorts of things spinning out of control. I see people's lives caught up in this tornado of time. My work is the numerical evaluation of social and consumer projections.

If what you told me is true, I can tell you that over fifty percent of the American population will die of sickness and disease from malnutrition or contaminated food products or lack of medicines. Diabetic medicines alone would affect twenty-nine, point one percent of American population. With a currency collapse I can easily see stagflation and violence at fifty percent and suicides will go off the chart. When you and grandpa said millions would die, you. . . Are you seriously

118

telling me. . ." Lydia threw up her hands and paced away a few steps, talking to herself out loud, "I am talking to someone God has allowed to come back from the grave. Of course, she's serious."

Lydia walked back to the bench next to grandma and flopped down with her head staring at the dirt floor. "Grandma, in your letter about the Angel. The Angel didn't have a choice, did she?" Grandma sat down beside her, "No child, she didn't. In the letter, I had to tell you the truth but I couldn't scare you.

You had to come of your own free will and I could not use fear to motivate your action. The Bible calls that witchcraft and conjuring. Conjuring up fear to exercise control over you. The Bible also says that twenty five percent of the earth's population will die in one generation of time, that much we know. Jesus also says that people will be getting married and partying right up to the very day just like in the days of Noah.

So, we know that there is a singular event on a singular day. You see, in Noah's time, it had never rained. Dew came down nightly to water the earth so when Noah told them about rain and a great flood, they laughed. They didn't know what it looked like. What Grandpa and I are telling you is the same way. You don't have anything to compare this to. You don't know what it looks like. What does a depression look like? What does the collapse of all fiat currencies look like? What does fourteen years of famine and disease look like? Think about this for a moment, Noah's brothers and sisters were beating on the side of the ark, trying to get in as the rains fell. As the water rose up through the city streets, women grabbed their babies and ran to the ark. But the Bible says, 'God shut the door'. Think how Noah must have felt listening to the cries and begs for mercy as those women held their babies above the water until they could no longer save themselves and both mothers and babies, brothers and sisters pounded on the ark as what was foretold had now come upon them.

Did Noah hear the cries of his nieces and nephews? Babies screams? How did he live with that? Did the sounds of their pounding on the ark haunt him like the pounding of his heart?

Lydia, there is a dark cloud on the horizon of your generation. I see it and I say it is going to be a catastrophic storm. You see it and say, 'I think it'll be fine. The economists say they can adjust the tax rates to stimulate the currency flow.' My child, both my opinion and your opinion have absolutely no bearing on the truth. Truth is truth, all by its self. What our opinions do have bearing on is how we prepare.

Faith is the Ark. Faith is a pragmatic functioning Ark. It's walls, foundation and sails are solid and can carry as many as you can get in. How many you can teach to walk by faith and save for the Lord is left up to you and what the church will look like in the next age will be entirely upon you and your generation.

You must become a Faith Coach and teach others to become Faith Coaches. And not this new age flippant style of church going faith, being taught today." Tears began to drop to the dirt floor, "Grandma, this is so much bigger than me. Who am I but a drop of water in an ocean?" Grandma caressed Lydia's shoulders, "Child, you are the Lord's seed of Trust and Faith. You and your generation will manifest the greatness of the Church for generations to come. Right now, you see a gigantic problem and a small you but that will change very

120

soon.

Are you ready to start today's studies?" Lydia looked up to see grandma's smiling face and sparkling eyes, "The Angel didn't have a choice. I guess I better get ready." Grandma took my hand and down the aisle, at a brisk pace, we went.

"First let's cover aquaponic gardening. See these plants growing in gravel?" Lydia looked down at the grow bed, "Wow. They are growing in rocks. I hadn't noticed that before. How does that work?" Grandma pointed, "Child, this is the gardening of the future. Actually, it is now being accepted around the world because it is a closed system." Lydia looked up, "Closed system?" Grandma continued, "Yes, closed system. It does not need any fertilizers, plant foods or pesticides.

Have you ever had an aquarium as you were growing up?" Lydia nodded yes. "Then you know exactly how this works. In your aquarium you had a charcoal filter that water went through to purify it. That is what this gravel bed is to that large fish tank over there. We have a fish feeder set up on a dusk and dawn solar powered timer that spreads feed to the fish. The fish process the food into waste that is pumped to the gravel grow beds also at dusk and dawn. Then the fish waste becomes the plant nutrients and the purified water returns to the tank. Simple closed system.

If you fertilize or spray the plants you will kill the fish. Lydia, this system can be done in an apartment and supply a family with year-round fresh food. There is a little to learn about the amount of fish to the amount of gravel and how much food to feed the fish, but you can quickly get that on your own." Lydia walked over to the tank, "There are a lot of fish in here." Grandma smiled, "Yes ma'am, my little lady. Never did like to do things small. For every pound of fish, we get fourteen pounds of plant food items. We harvest the fish twice a year and totally clean the tank before starting up a new bunch. I always did like fishing, never had a problem catching one for supper any time I liked."

We both giggled. "Now, young lady, let's step outside and show you a few things you will have to know how to do." Once outside, we went to the lower side of the greenhouse, away from the house. There were several cabinet style boxes with windows on them.

Grandma started explaining, "These are our solar dehydrators. They are really, really simple to make." grandma reached over and opened up one of the cabinet doors. "See these screens? They are the same screens as on most windows in everyone's house. Feel the heat in here." Lydia stuck her arm inside. "That's really warm. What is that on the screen?"

Grandma pulled out a screen to look, "Plantain seeds on that tray, this one is Evening Primrose seeds and that one is Jerusalem Artichoke. Which one do you want to learn about first?" Lydia smiled, "I guess the artichoke." Grandma pulled out a root that looked like a small potato or a ginger root, "Even though it's called an artichoke, it isn't. It is, actually related to the sunflower and grows about nine feet tall, has a yellow flower that looks half like a daisy and half like a small sun flower. The root is what you want, here taste." Grandma sliced a small thin piece and handed it to Lydia. "That's really good! Taste like a mix between a potato and a peanut." Grandma took a nibble as well, "Yeah, and you can't kill these things. Don't plant these where you have anything else, you can forget it. Each tuber makes fourteen other tubers per year and then dies.

Each of them make fourteen and so on. Harvest them after the frost so all the nutrients in the stem has returned to the root. Slice them thin and add them to your salads. They are made of inulin which is good for treating diabetes and good for low starch diets. It aids in probiotics and multiplies the good flora in your digestion system, helps fight candida yeast, heartburn, high blood pressure and rheumatism. The juice from the root is a good sugar substitute."

Lydia reached on to the next tray, "And this was?" "Plantain seeds", grandma responded, "That's a power house. This one heals wounds, is a body purifier, congestion aid and neutralizer of poisons and toxic elements. Is used for skin diseases, constipation, digestion, prostrate, urinary, respiratory, fevers, infections and hay fever. Protects the mucus membranes from inflammation and calms the muscle contractions in asthma, colic and stomach aches. The tannins in plantain are astringent and is useful in treating tuberculosis, stomach ulcers, bowel hemorrhaging, blood vomiting, diarrhea, colitis, colon inflammation, hemorrhoids and helps with excessive menstrual bleeding. Helps clear stomach and bowel infections, peptic ulcers and urinary tract infection. It was used in the Civil War to stop bleeding in the field. The leaf tea is good for sore throat, dilating bronchial and breathing issues. It contains all eighteen amino acids. Dry the leaves, powder them and use them in your soups year-round. Lydia, I believe you will find Plantain in almost every person's yard in America except those that spray to kill broad leaf plants.

God is so gracious, most people are walking on top of the very medicine they need, in their own yards." She slid the tray back in and pulled out the next, "This is Evening Primrose, also known as the King's Cure-All. In your life time, this will be the leading treatment for breast cancer. It has the essential Omega fatty acids, including the GLA that the body does not make. It prevents hardening of the arteries, high blood pressure, lowers cholesterol and helps balance sex hormones, both estrogen and testosterone. Helps with PMS and menopause, diabetes, nervous system, asthma, cough, migraines, bowel pain and prostrate issues. If you pick the seed pods before they flower, they are like tiny okra. But each plant has hundreds on them. The seed pods have hundreds of tiny seed. You can eat the whole plant but I just add the seeds to my turkey dinners, dressings and casseroles." Lydia reached out her hand for a few seeds, "Grandma, those are so tiny, it would take a hundred to cover a penny."

Grandma returned the tray, "That is what makes it so simple to maintain health. I'm not changing your diet, just adding to it some of the simplest things to harvest. Even if you eat very poorly, the body will respond to these. Can I give you a short story that may help you to understand health and healing a little better?" Lydia eagerly responded, "Oh yes Ma'am."

Grandma walked over to a pine tree and began, "There was a boy who hurt his foot and went to a doctor to get help. The doctor was very good and soon the boy was all better. The boy went to the same church as the doctor and one day the young boy was bragging on the doctor to some of the people in the church. Upon overhearing the young boy, the doctor came into the conversation to help the boy to understand healing. 'Young man, doctors do not heal. God does. What the doctor does is correct the environment and God does the rest. For instance, if you had a broken arm, the doctor would set the bone in place, correct the environment, splint it and God would do the healing. If you have a stomach issue, we try to identify and correct the chemical environment and God does the healing.'

So, what these plants do is help correct and maintain a healthy system or environment. Most folks wait until they are sick then want a medicine or treatment to relieve pain, of which, these plants do. But more than relieving pain, these plants create a healthy environment. It's like one of the college students said to Elizabeth last week, 'Hard to build something out of play dough if ain't no play dough in the house.'"

Lydia walked down the rows of dehydrators. "Grandma, there are thirty dehydrators here. Why so many?" Grandma motioned Lydia to come to her, "Because we house thirty interns per quarter and each have to learn to build and inventory needs per season.

Can you grow grass?" Lydia looked at her to see if it was a trick question, "Of course. Why would you ask that?" Grandma started, "If people can grow grass, why can't they grow beans?" Lydia thought, "I guess they could, if they would." "Well child, my point being that when times change, agriculture will instantly become a necessity and if you have seeds, you're set.

Dehydrated beans and corn last for twenty-five years, Just, bucket them as air tight as you can and no need for electricity. All grasses are edible but wheat and barley are the best. Now, let me tell you how to build a simple dehydrator. Take a cardboard box. Put a two-inch hole in the bottom on one side and a two-inch hole in the top on the other side. Put a cup or a glass in each corner and lay a screen on them. Then place a window or something clear on top of the box and put it in the sunshine. Slice you a few grapes or fruit and put on the screen, then enjoy them that evening. There you go, you graduated dehydration.

Okay, what tree is this?" Lydia looked up at it, "It's a Pine tree." Grandma smiled, "That's what you call it but the Indians called it the Healing Tree. First, all pine trees are edible. The whole thing, needles, the small cones that contain the pollen, the inner bark can be eaten raw, dried, powdered, steamed or boiled. One pound of inner bark has more nutrients than nine cups of raw whole milk. The resin can be chewed like gum for B vitamins and helps with lung conditions.

The pine tree is the best source for vitamin C in the world. The pine needles have three hundred times more vitamin C than oranges and also contains natural turpentine which helps pneumonia and bronchitis. The root bark can be soaked and the water drank for sugar water. The pine nuts are an outstanding source of protein but the pine pollen is a story all by its self.

Pine Pollen is a complete and ultimate super food. A complete food and medicine that contains over two hundred bioactive nutrients, minerals and vitamins in one serving that is completely absorbed by the human body. There is not any other supplement that can do that.

Pine Pollen will restore testosterone levels, build muscle mass, keep skin tight and smooth, breast health for women, regenerate tissue and burn off excess fat. It is a super-food and affects the entire body and organs, as well as stabilizes collagen and elastin, which make up the underlying matrix of the skin. Balance hormones and counters the effects of estrogen mimicking substances in our plastic bottles, food containers, medications and lotions. Increases sexual powers of both men and women and is completely digestible." Lydia just stared as grandma picked up a cane machete and chopped off a large chunk of bark,

"Lydia, see this white inner bark? This is not only edible but is used as a wound dressing. Pine sap is a bandage for small cuts. Not only does it stick the skin together, it has all the nutrients to correct the environment, as the doctor said, and that is why the Indians called it the healing tree. Larger bandages or casts are made with this inner bark.

And of course, the pine nuts are a great food. The Indians made pine nut soup as a replacement for mother's milk. Need I say more?" Lydia looked up at the tree and then back to grandma, "Why haven't we been taught this in school?" Grandma shook her head as she walked over to another tree, "Commerce over conscience, my child.

Commerce over conscience. Capitalism is how we do business, it is not who we are. But, when every decision you make is based solely on revenues, you have lost your soul to the god of money.

Lydia, we have covered a few plants, wild carrots, a couple of grasses and two trees, the Moringa and the Pine. We have covered aquaponic gardening, solar dehydrators and the shelf life of corn and beans. Look down through these woods. How many different trees and plants do you see?" Lydia looked in all directions, pausing slightly, seeming to count in her head, "Hundreds upon hundreds, Grandma."

"My child, God is able to do exceedingly, abundantly, above all you can ask or think. There are five people groups that live over one hundred and twenty years and they do not live in America. In fact, America is 49th in life expectancy in the world and we have an infant mortality rank of 46th among the nations of the world and that does not include abortions. We no longer lead the world in anything except incarcerations. And if a tree is known by the fruit it bears, we do not even lead in our Christian faith and the American medical system is a business not a science.

Just in child birth, they are starting to take the children at least two weeks early so it will be classified as a premature baby thus allowing them to bill the government for the child's health care. And to make it worse, they give the child medicine to remove the digestive acids in the stomach so the child will weigh less than normal, in order to keep the government paying for the child's health costs for two years.

Lydia, every sickness or disease is directly related to the foods you eat and, or the lack of one or more nutrients in the internal environment or sin. We have covered over-population as a farce and demonstrated that the food source is greater than man can remotely consume. Just look at these trees here. The Poplar tree inner bark has all the vitamins and minerals the body will ever need from the cradle to the grave and it is on every continent.

The Peach bark is for memory and fatigue, eye health, cardiac arrhythmia, ringing in the ears and a hundred other items. The persimmon tree takes care of spider veins and varicose veins. The powdered leaves bind to fat in the body and is for weight loss." Lydia and grandma had walked down the garden path to a bench, "Grandma, it is like my eyes have just been opened to a complete new world.

I have been in the world but I was completely blind to

128

God's world. When you said that humans were the only creature that had to pay to occupy earth and that was not how God planned it, you weren't kidding.

I can literally walk outside my door and have everything I need if I just understood what each plant was for." Grandma had a big smile, "Yes child, there isn't one that God didn't put here on purpose. As darkness moves closer and closer, it would serve you well to study the plants more and more.

Child, there is a habit I would like you to develop." I knew it would have to be a good one so I said, "I bet I'm going to like it too." She smiled, "The habit is, 'Eat one, Seed one'. If people would just take the seeds from what they ate each day and plant them along a road somewhere, in one generation the abundance would feed the world. If you eat an apple, take the seeds that day and put them in the dirt. An orange, pear, bean, corn, if we just seeded every day, regardless of weather or season, abundance would overtake us.

The best watermelon I ever had was the ones that grew around our animal pens. We would give them our rinds and the seeds would just get trampled into the dirt. Next year, we had plants. I threw a rotten tomato into the edge of the woods and next year, there was a fabulous tomato vine."

Lydia thought for a moment about what she had eaten in the past week or so that she could have planted. "Grandma, just imagining what I have eaten in the last week, that would be a lot of plants growing somewhere." "Yes child. Just plant them in a park or by a lake if you don't have a yard, or along a road somewhere. Just make it a habit to never throw a seed in the trash. A seed is a future." Grandma reached into her coat pocket and pulled out a dark colored seed.

"The Bible talks a lot about seeds. Let me show you why. See this apple seed? If I give you this seed, I am giving you the ability to grow a tree. Not only that but I am giving you the ability to feed yourself. Also, within that one seed you, have the ability, to feed your whole family. Let's not stop there actually, within that one seed is the ability to feed your whole town by taking the seeds from the apples your tree grows and growing more trees. Realistically, within that one seed I just gave you, is the ability to feed the whole world but only according to the power within you.

Eat one, Seed one, would be a good habit to adopt and teach. It doesn't take very much time but it would require you to think about others and the future. Lydia, you and everyone you equip to become a Faith Coach is a God Seed." Lydia took the seed and took her heal and dug in the dirt, put the seed in the hole and covered it with her foot. "Grandmother, I'll do that. That makes a lot of sense."

Grandma smiled, "Let's cover three more things for today. First, planting depth for any seed is the thickness of the seed. So, the apple seed is about a quarter of an inch. It would be planted the same. One quarter inch in depth." Lydia nodded.

"Second let's walk to this end of the greenhouse." As they rounded the north end of the greenhouse, Lydia saw five black plastic barrels with fabric cloth and plywood covering each top with a small board separating the plywood from the fabric so whatever was in the barrels could breath. "Grandma, what's that smell?" Grandma lifted off one of the plywood lids and then removed the rubber band holding the cloth, "Vinegar my child, Apple Cider vinegar.

Do you know how to make it?" Lydia shook her head no.
130

"Okay, this one is really tough. Pick up the apples off the ground, good ones, bad ones and all of them daily as they fall. crush them and throw them, juice and all, in the barrel or bucket then cover the barrel with a cloth and secure it. On top of that place a board or stick as a spacer, then put a rain cap on top of the stick and put a brick or something on top of the plywood so the wind won't blow it off. Come back in the spring and strain off the vinegar. Real hard, isn't it?"

Lydia leaned over to smell inside the barrel, "Whoa, that is strong but I can smell it's vinegar. Why so much?" Grandma replaced the coverings. "Vinegar is used to pickle a lot of our foods, for making cheese, it is the base for many of our home remedies and it is all we use to clean with. It will kill all unwanted insects and will kill unwanted grass or weeds. When the darkness comes, you will need this knowledge, for sure." With a serious face Lydia responded, "I can remember this.

Now, you said three things. What was the third?" Grandma turned and looked at Lydia, "In the greenhouse, you said God had allowed me to come back from the grave." Again, Lydia nodded. "Dead people are in the grave, I am alive, I came from Heaven." We both laughed.

"When you get the diaries, Mother Mary will tell you what Heaven is like. There isn't any way I can tell you what it's like. It is beyond my words but Her diary will open your mind and fill your spirit so you will understand what waits for you."

They entered the greenhouse from the end door and made their way to the middle of the house. "Lydia, you need to get some rest and I'll be here in the morning. Tomorrow is my last day with you and we will be covering a lot." They hugged and Lydia went out the main door. She looked back just as she started to step outside, grandma was gone.

Chapter Seven

Sunset

The afternoon was pleasant. Everyone was still in the main house as I returned from the greenhouse. They had not left there since my last meeting with them and they were about to bust. Needless-to-say, they wanted to know every word and I felt more than glad to share it all. It seemed to feel like the tornado had left but I wasn't real sure if I still had my sanity.

I went upstairs after supper and sat on the balcony to watch the sunset. My mind raced back to Grandpa's words the night before, "Plagues, judgment coming to the White House, famine, the four horses, 666." Then naturally I cross referenced that with what Grandma said today, "major attacks on American soil and the collapse of all the fiat currencies." I wondered how they came up with these predictions.

I thought about Mom and what her life would be like. Then I thought about Grandma Grace and grandpa John. It kind of felt like they would be fine. My mind jumped to Grandma Fayth. I chuckled, I knew there wasn't anything that could stop her. I knew that both Grandma Grace and Grandma Fayth had learned all the things I was now being taught, so they knew the world was God's house and they knew their way around inside it.

I thought about Robert. He was probably packing his things by now. I wondered what life without him would be like. For the first time since I've known him, I saw the value of having a strong partner. I had never looked at him as an equal and surely not as a partner. I wondered for a while if he would believe me about what was coming. Deep down inside, I knew he would and he would also have his hand on the ball and his head in the game. My rational side tried to kick in, "what am I saying? Have I lost my mind? This can't be happening. Surely this is just a dream." Nope, didn't work. Couldn't get myself to reattach to the world I belonged to just a few days ago.

I realized that I was hopelessly and helplessly on this journey and I had better become a quick learner. As the sun set and the sky displayed an array of color, I looked toward the east and saw the moon climbing the mountain. I thought about how its beautiful glow was just borrowed light from the sun. I wondered if faith was like that? As I watched it rise and pondered its glory, I thought about how knowledge was like the light of the moon and that all man did was reflect what we learn. Just some reflect it better than others. I seemed to become energized like a researcher on the edge of a breakthrough.

Questions for grandpa just started popping into my head and I went to the nightstand and started writing them down. I must have been caught up in thought because I didn't realize it had already become dark by the time I looked up from my papers. I thought about grandpa and went to the balcony door

. "Good evening Mrs. Lydia Fayth. Excellent evening to discuss the logos of God", He said from the high-backed vine rocking chair. "Grandpa, I couldn't wait for you to get here. I have so much to ask you." I took my place in the rocker next to him. He smiled and said, "Fire away." I glanced at my notes, so many questions, "I'm trying to organize the questions into some kind of order but, here goes.

I don't know enough about church but from the outside looking in, it appears that it has lost connection to society. In college I was taught all the arguments from a Thomas Payne book, The Age of Reason. He seemed to be a logical man. He wrote the book 'Common Sense' which fostered the reason for the colonies to declare independence. And I believe he help write the framework for the Declaration. Was he wrong?"

Logical debate didn't seem to bother grandpa, "Yes and no. He believed in God but not the Son. That was because of a very poor presentation of the gospel from his uncle when Thomas was age nine. I would convince him the same way I will convince you.

You wake up tomorrow in a foreign land in a magnificent castle, with all the blessings and graces that one could imagine. What would you do and, or think?" I thought for a moment, "I guess I would try to find out where I was, how I got there and who owned the place."

He smiled and leaned forward a little, "Well then. Look at all those stars in the sky tonight. Look at the mountain in the moon light. Is that not a castle that you did not build?" I smiled, "I see but that doesn't undermine his argument." He started rocking but had a half smile like a cat who just trapped a mouse,

"Well Mrs. Payne, if you didn't build it, do you think you should at least follow the owner's rules? Mr. Payne's argument is based on the concept that he has a right to live in God's castle, rent free, without obligation, self-willed and self-right, making his own opinion God to himself. And that is because he is many generations removed from his original father.

Let me ask you. You lease out a house and the tenants do not live up to their obligations. Do their children, one, five or ten generations later have any rights to occupy your property? Did you build the earth or are you suggesting a big bang? Mr. Payne has already logically admitted that God has built the castle because he admires the book of Genesis and Psalms nineteen.

What he fails to admit is that man was disobedient and that there was and is a cost for it. He does ask a good question. 'Why would God give you vision to see stars millions of miles away, if he did not want you to study them?' Would it not have been better to only allow you to see short distances?

Why then does the church condemn the study of the stars when the bible says, 'The heavens declare the glory of God and the firmament sheweth his handywork. Day unto day uttereth speech and night unto night sheweth knowledge. There is no speech nor language where their voice is not heard. Their line is gone out through all the earth, and their words to the end of the world. In them hath he set a tabernacle for the sun.'

Mr. Payne, like so many other people and religions, try to do away with sin or transgression and thusly eliminating the need for a savior." I sat there for a minute trying to form a logical argument but came up blank. I looked back at my notes,

"Okay grandpa, I guess the rest of my questions fall into two categories, prophecy and purpose. First let me ask you about prophesy. How do you and grandma know these things and how can I know them for sure? Is there some kind of secret code in the Bible or do these events just drop into your head during prayer and dreams?

I must say that I have been directly communicated within, both of these areas, in the past couple of days." Grandpa stood up and walked to the railing, "Look at the shadows in the front garden. Can you tell me what time it is?" I stood up and walked to the rail.

"On my goodness! I never looked at the garden in the moonlight. That is gorgeous. Look at all those angel statues. They cast different length shadows but seem to all be pointing at something. What does it all mean?"

Grandpa began, "Lydia, have you ever seen a sun calendar?" "I have seen sundials but I'm not sure what a sun calendar is", I said. He continued, "A sun calendar is a sundial that cast a shadow at noon and a rock or marker is placed each day at the point of the shadow. In-the-course-of 365 days, it will have 181 stones in a straight line. One would place a larger stone at the spring and fall equinox and if the sun was up, you could look to your calendar and easily determine what day it was and what season it was."

Being a human calculator, I quickly recognized something wrong, "181 doubled only gives you 362 days. You're missing 3 days.", I said with a kinda of, 'gotcha grin'.

He smiled, "You're really good but that proves I know something you don't. You, number your days on paper and one integer has no greater value than another. But, the Heavens declare the work of his hand.

Have you ever heard of, 'Dies Natalis Solis Invicti', the 'Birthday of the Unconquered Sun'?" I am sure I looked puzzled, "Not really." He explained, "December 21st is the winter solstice and it is when the sun cast the longest shadow. It also remains at its lowest point for three days before beginning to rise again on December 25th. Many cultures felt that the Sun died for three days and would rise again on the third day.

Now, I am sure you have heard that the Son of God remained three days in the tomb and rose back to life on the third day. Did you think December 25th was just a good idea for Christ Mass? The Heavens declare the Glory of God."

I just shook my head, "Okay grandpa, I'm out of my league. What's next?" He smiled and pointed toward the garden, "What you are looking at is the round calendar. Time can be told by the sun and moon, but much, much more than that, ages, stages, seasons, patterns, oracles and events are all there for everyone to see. It is unfortunate that the devil has blinded the church and wisdom has been locked out."

I looked at the shadows, "Grandpa, what does it all mean? How can I understand?" He began, "Lydia, God did not give us enough time to teach it all. Just enough time to give you the foundations. The diaries will give you a lot more, but even they do not teach you the tapestry of time. Can I give you a wagon load of information, most of which will stretch your belief system and then expect you to continue the study and learn as you grow?"

"Yes sir.", I responded. "Well then, first you must learn about ages and stages. A day is a unit of time calculated by the revolution of the Earth and is measured by the Sun. The seasons are also units of time as well as a year. All of which are measured by the Sun. There are stages and seasons of life that are also units of time but they are measured by what God told Job was 'Mazzaroth'.

A stage of life is 2648 days which is 7.25 years. Every seven years or so, you will go through a major restructuring.

Just examine your own life, at age seven it would have been school, family or health. Again, at age fourteen and a half, maturity, family or health. By age twenty-one, almost twenty-two, school, job, career or health. Buying cars, marriage for some, having babies for others.

All this restructuring occurs at the beginning of these stages of life. Then at age twenty-nine, most people feel like all of hell and half of heaven has just found out who they are. That is, you, right now, because a season of life is twenty-nine years. You have four stages per season and if you live wisely, then you should have four seasons of life.

As a person examines life, they will find that each of the four stages seem to repeat themselves in each season. If a woman chased men at the twenty-one, stage of life, or a man chased women at the twenty-one, stage, they will find themselves facing similar challenges around age fifty. I'm sure you have seen men wearing gold necklaces on grey haired chest, driving their sports cars."

He chuckled as he sat back down in the rocker. "I sure have.", I couldn't help but laugh. He continued, "Grandma and I knew a lady school teacher who hit fifty and it went ugly. Problem was, she got the same result that she had at age twenty-one. Meeting and attracting the same type fellows.

God has designed this pattern and if we learn from life and others, then we do not have to repeat the class, but if you are extremely self-willed, you generally go around again.

Faith is the substance of things hoped for, if you do not know what you want then you will be led by carnal desires and emotional appetites thusly repeating the previous pattern.

Abraham learned, King David learned, Moses learned., these are great examples of the seasons and cycles of life. Jesus went to the dessert at age twenty-nine, knowing full well that the devil would be there to tempt him.

So, this wisdom will help you navigate life and, also help you know when to help someone else." I seem to think out loud, "Know when to help?" He paused knowing his statement would generate a question. "If you have a sixteen, year old, with a tank full of gas and a pocket full of money, they are not going to hear a word you are saying. They may be pleasant, attentive and even some what eager, but it will produce no fruit. They are not at a changing point, but you teach that same person at age twenty to twenty-two, you will alter the course of their and their children's lives forever.

The same goes for any changing point of any stage. You have maturity cycles in life as well. From birth to age five is a training cycle, they are trained to walk, trained to talk and much, much more. From age five to fifteen is the teaching cycle where they load the brain with both good and bad information. Followed by the identity cycle from fifteen to twenty-five, where they try to find a place in life.

They try to establish who they are and this cycle is like the roller coaster of life, up one minute, down the next, up one week, down the next. Because they were not taught how to live by faith, they don't know what a faith plan or a faith map is. They make good and bad choices because that is what their brain is full of. Most are taught that having fun with their friends is the objective of life and most have children during this time, go in debt and divorce, just to name a few.

Ninety percent crash land on planet earth at this stage and

then, twenty-five to forty is the recovery stage. They know what doesn't work but are not sure what does. The one thing they know for sure is they are not doing that again. Many spend this stage of life just trying to untie the mess they tangled themselves up to.

Then comes the 'significant stage', forty to sixty-five. Pride always comes before the fall and by god they are going to be important during this stage, no matter who they have to hurt. They may be a quiet person but be careful, they will stab you in the back in order to make themselves look good. Somehow, by the grace of God, many make it to their 'contribution stage'.

Sixty-five to ninety becomes a time to give back and that brings them differing levels of joy or comfort. Many still do this as a self-centered way of being important. Self-worship has no place in Heaven and God does not allow it. Now, 'that being said', each person differs based on knowledge and spirit."

As I stared at the round calendar, I looked closer at each of the angel statues. They were all different and all women. There were thirteen with two standing back to back with swords in each hand. I saw the one like cupid with the bow and arrow and the lady with a water urn turned downward. There was one plowing with an ox, one holding a balance pole across her shoulders with a water bucket on each end, one look mean, like a devil with a pointy tail. One sitting with her foot in the water and one in the water fountain. Another holding up a fish toward the sky and one holding a child, one had a set of horns and the other held up a heart shaped crystal in one hand. Each cast a shadow, some longer than others and the crystal seemed to cast a laser type light that moved with the moon.

"Grandpa, I am sure you have, some kind of system to

understand all this but it all feels Greek to me." He turned toward me. "Greek? No child, this is Hebrew. If the Heavens declare the work of His hands, then we must use the Hebrew text and culture to understand what the writers are trying to teach us."

I guess I was getting a little frustrated, "We're going to have to graduate me tonight. So far, I know nothing more about famines, diseases, or anything you and grandma have spoken about. How do we get there?"

He smiled briefly but it was followed by a look of a battle harden general. "Okay, we finally broke through the feely faith and your spirit requires meat. I think we can get there from here. In order for you to understand the tapestry of time, the events we have spoken of, you first have to see the round calendar.

Look at the garden. Can you see the circle?" I looked back at the angels. As I stared, there appeared to be on a stone walkway that made a complete circle. "I see the walkway the Angels are on." "Okay. Look closely at the walkway. Do you see the four large crystal stones?" He stepped closer to the balcony rail. I followed along. "Yes Sir. I do." He pointed, "See the one closes to us? That is the winter stone. See the shadow touching it?

Now, look at each stone in the walkway. There are three hundred and sixty stone and each Angel watches over thirty steps. Now, beyond that circle is a much larger circle. Do you see it?" I looked and looked. I just couldn't see it. "I don't see it." He pointed again, "See the boarder stone on the driveway that circle the garden?" I felt a chill run through me but there wasn't a breeze. "I see it! And I see different color stones in a

142

lot of places around the circle. Okay, so-far I can see a round calendar year and I can divide it up into four seasons.

Now what?" "Here is where you meet wisdom. First, answer me one question. What is the purpose of knowledge?" He leaned against the rail looking at me. I stared back at him kind of looking for a sign. He didn't give. "To learn? Power? To increase one's ability? I don't know what you are looking for."

He crossed his arms. "To learn for what? Power for what? Increased ability for what?" I felt pressured and I didn't like the way it felt. "I'm the student. For what?" He smiled, "Knowledge always has a purpose. Knowledge is for navigation. The Ark of Faith has to travel through time and you have to know how to navigate.

Never forget the purpose of knowledge is navigation.

If you are going nowhere, you do not need it. Faith is the substance of things hoped for. Knowledge is not the objective, in and of its self. There must be an objective. Now, who are the Angels?" I looked back again. "Grandpa, don't get mad at me but are they the zodiacs?" He didn't appear effected by the question. "Yes. Now, why the second circle?" I glanced back, "I'm clueless."

He motioned for me to follow him as he went for the stairs at the far end of the balcony. We made our way to the driveway. "Lydia, stand on the walkway at the shadows point." I walked over and stood on the stone. "Your shadow is now touching a stone in the outer circle. Do you see which one?"

I looked and it was easy to see. "I see it. Now what?" He pointed toward it. "Go look at it and you tell me." I walked to it and there was something wrote on it. 'Polis'. "It says 'Polis'.

What does that mean?" He motioned me toward a bench. "Polis is a fortunate star portending success, ambition and truthfulness. This star shows up with almost the regal qualities of mighty Regulus which is one of the four horses in Revelations.

Polis is the only star that will indicate more of the high office in spiritual life, Preacher, Teacher, Bishop or at least a prominent Theologian. If Polis is unfavorably challenged, it may show more of a self-styled pretender.

Mrs. Lydia Faith, you do not have any unfavorable challengers and in two days from now, Pluto joins the Sun or should I say, Power joins your Soul. Pluto is the planet of power and death. In scripture he is called the Angel of Death and also the Pride of Life. You will die to self but a seed must die to be released."

I just stared at the angels, the circles and back at the name on the stone. "Grandpa, does this calendar show you everything about me?" "Yes." "Then this calendar tells you events in other people's lives?" "Yes. But also in businesses, marriages, partnerships, governments, and much, much more. And as you weave all these together you form a tapestry of time that allows you to see a much larger picture.

It has all been here for ages just waiting for appointed people at the appointed times." I looked back at the larger circle, "Grandpa, what are the outer stones and how are they used?" He looked up to heaven for a moment, as if he was double checking with God. "Mrs. Lydia, what is the exact time on your watch?" I felt the question odd but looked down at my watch, "Eleven, fifty." He continued, "How many hands does your watch have?" I looked again, even though I knew my watch did not have a second hand, "Just two."

He stood up and I followed. "Can you tell me which Angel has the moon right now?" I looked back to where the shadows were, "All of them are casting shadows but the one holding the crystal heart has the shadow of the cross on it. The cross in the center of the water fountain."

He smiled really big and it seemed to change the atmosphere. " Very good. The shadow is at nine degrees in the heart and we are dealing with heart issues. The very core of wisdom and time is the very thing life is made of. Your time piece has two hands, this time piece has ten. You have seen from the balcony the Sun keeps us aware of the hours, days, months and seasons. Now you see that the moon also travels around the table of time.

The Bible says, 'And God made two great lights; the greater light to rule the day, and the lesser light to rule the night: he made the stars also.' To 'rule' does not mean to measure. It means to exercise dominion and power. And as you have seen so far, the placement of the Sun indicates your external path to be moving into ministry.

The Moon indicates your internal path is the core or heart of the matter. As I said earlier, you have no unfavorable challenges to your Sun path. Your Sun and Moon are joined in favor. Many people get divided in life and you will always find that their Sun or external life, is in conflict, with their Moon or internal life. You have been taught from kindergarten to keep time with a clock and a calendar but time is circular with ten calendars, each with overlapping seasons of differing lengths."

I just stood there looking at all the stones in the outer

ring. "Okay Grandpa, let's get to the point. Show me an upcoming event in America. How does this calendar do that?" He smiled as we walked around the pavers.

"First, when was America born?" He looked at me for an answer. "I would say, July 4th, 1776." He continued, "You are correct and actually July 4th, 1776 at 5:12 in the afternoon, in Philadelphia, Pennsylvania. That would be where their calendar would begin, so, let's start at twelve degrees Archer and place each of our ten, time pieces to see where they point."

It took about two hours for grandpa to walk me through the calendar of events. As he walked me through two hundred years of history, event by event and demonstrating that each of the time pieces clearly and accurately indicated each event prior to it happening, I stood in the calendar of time, with the pieces set to November 29th, 2015 at 3:57 pm. Grandpa looked at me with a solemn face, "Child, what will you be doing on this day?"

I shook my head. By now I did not have words. He began, Pride and Death cross the threshold and enters the house of finance, Satan and Soul are crossing into darkness on the heart of the scorpion. Look at the stone in the outer circle. It is Oriel, the watcher of the West. Antares, the Red horse!

Child, I do not expect you to comprehend the term, 'Fear of the Lord', but Hebrews 11:7 said Noah build the Ark because of it. I could spend a week describing this to you and still not adequately translate all that is going to begin on this day in time. The Arch Angel Oriel, the Watcher of the West will be sent to Judge. The Royal Star is Red, so there is no doubt a season of war has arrived. Satan has captured the Soul of the West and rides the Heart of the Scorpion across the horizon of darkness. Satan will rule the fourteen and one-half years of fall and winter, and the judgment of the Darwinites shall famine the earth.

Oriel announces the beginning of Darkness and the loss of freedom. A government for the government is born, and the people mourn. Child, you are in the bottleneck of this event. Will the people repent? I would not come into your bedroom with you last night, even to get a piece of paper but today mothers and sisters lie down with their infant and toddler male children and even their infant and toddler grandchildren. Fathers and brothers lie with their infant and toddler daughters, sisters and granddaughters. This is not only tolerated, it is encouraged is some parts of America.

Sex is the number one motivator of conduct and commerce in America. Not since the prophet Balaam has the sins of the Moabites filled the earth as it has in America and think not that the King of Heaven and Earth has lost His arm of judgment."

I stared at each time piece and their placement. I looked at each of the outer stones that lined up with each piece. I realized I had tears coming down my face. I turned toward grandpa, He was gone! I looked all around but he really wasn't there.

"Now what Lord? Here I stand, in the calendar of time, who am I?" I walked around for hours looking at the names on each of the outer stones. I realized it would take a lifetime of study to unravel Grandpa's Tapestry of Time but at the same time, I felt that grandpa trapped me on purpose because he knew that I had an analytic mind and that I couldn't taste this much truth and not understand the recipe.

147

I made my way back to my room, said my prayers, thanking God for everything I wanted to be here tomorrow, then asked him how I was supposed to make a difference and fell into his care as I went to sleep.

The Second Dream

I woke to the sound of somebody at my balcony door. It was bright outside but dark inside my room. I looked at the door as I heard the sound, of the door knob. I knew something wasn't right about this, every nerve in my body was alive but, yet, I seemed paralyzed.

Suddenly I saw it! It was a huge man-like shadow! Completely dark but completely three dimensional. It was a complete man but in a shadow form. It was trying to get into my room and I was frozen in fear. I tried to scream but nothing would come out! My heart was pounding and I could hear the glass in the door shaking violently but the door wouldn't open.

It was so bright outside that I could clearly see the man but so dark in my room that I could not see anything but the door. It moved to open the door again and the glass rattled so bad that I covered my head as I tried to scream. I tried to pray, "God please help me!".

I was instantly in a room lit by candles. My heart was still racing and I could hardly catch my breath. I felt safe but the room was strange. There was a concrete type table about twenty steps in front of me. The air was dry and I felt a little warm. There was a person in a white robe standing behind the concrete table. He pointed toward the floor between us and I saw a car driving on a major highway.

Suddenly, I was in the car, hovering at the ceiling, between the front and back seats on the passenger side. There was a pretty lady driving and she was praying out loud. 'Lord, please, oh please heal my mother.' As soon as she said the words, a box rose up from the car and as I followed, it came to rest upon the concrete table in front of the man in the robe.

As he opened the box, I could see an elderly gray-haired lady who was in a hospital. She had tubes running to her arms and a mask on her face. Something drew my attention to the doorway off to my right and in it, a couple of steps hidden, was the shadow thing that had come to my room.

My heart started to race again. The man in the robe raised his hand and it caught my attention as he pointed back toward the car. The lady had made it to work and backed her car into the parking place. She turned off the car, took out the keys and place both hands on top of the steering wheel, placing her head against her hands, she began to pray.

I was inside the car as she began, 'I beg you, oh Lord, please heal my mother. I know I don't deserve anything but I'm begging you, please.'. As soon as she prayed, I was instantly back at the concrete table. The shadow figure of the man came out the door and crossed in front of the table. He stopped, picked up the box and said, "This is Mine!", and carried the box out a door on the left.

I could feel anger rising-up inside of me like I had never felt. I saw the lady exit her car and walking to her job. I saw the elderly lady in the hospital and the shadow man was standing at her door. I was crying and screaming at the same time! I looked

149

at the man in the robe. He raised his arm and pointed out the door on the left and said, "Go. Get what belongs to Me!".

Chapter Eight

Grandma's Last Day

I jolted as I woke, scanning the room and quickly looked at the balcony door. It was daylight and it had been a dream. My heart was still pounding and I had dried tears on my face. I glanced at the clock as I headed for the shower but I stopped at the bathroom door. I still felt apprehensive, I turned and went to the balcony door. It was unlocked and I thought about the dream. I locked it, as well as the bedroom door and looked in both closets before getting into the shower.

As I passed through the kitchen, Elizabeth sensed something wasn't right. "Mrs. Lydia, you have a serious disposition this morning. You okay?" I drank my cup of coffee without sitting down and answered as I was headed for the back door, "It was a very, very long night. Grandpa loaded my wagon and I think the devil came to my room last night. I'll explain when I get in today."

The morning was overcast and moisture filled the air. It was warmer than normal but I recalled that I was on the east side of the house and the heater's exhaust exited through a rock bed under the deck. I entered the greenhouse not knowing what to think or feel. I was still fired up on the inside after being jerked around all night.

Grandma was tending plants in the center aisle as I came up. She turned and had a bright smile, "Happy Christmas Eve, my beautiful young lady". The sound of the words Christmas Eve pierced my mind. My world had been in a tornado for so long that Christmas had fallen off the map.

"Grandpa spoke about Christmas last night but it did not occur to me that it is here". Grandma leaned in for a hug, "Do you remember your early Christmases with your Dad and Mom"? I thought for a moment, I smiled as I thought of a special Christmas that Dad was home.

"Yes Ma'am. I sure do. But grandma, this is our last day and after last night, I think I'm in way over my head. I am absolutely outside my element. My comfort zone has now become a combat zone and I have lost all direction in life. Before your letter my focus was on my career, my desires and my needs. Now I can't find me or anything that resembles normal."

Grandma moved a few steps further down the aisle and continued to work plants. I realized that she was not going to respond. "You're not going to respond?" Grandma stood up and looked at me. "You haven't said anything that requires a response. What do you want?"

Without a thought I blurted, "My life back!" She didn't even raise her voice, "Then leave." She went back to working the plants. I headed for the door but made it as far as the first bench. I sat down and my mind raced through every word that had been said in the past few days. I must have sat there an hour or so before I saw grandmother's boots come up in front of me. I looked up and she smiled,

"Want to tell me about last night?" She sat down beside me, "Grandma, I'm scared. Grandpa walked me through two hundred years of factual history, event for event, and academically remove every foundation I thought to be solid. He then illuminated the next fifteen years of American history and left me standing in the center of the calendar, staring at a specific date and even named the exact time of the day. After hours of that I finally made it to bed and was woke by some huge shadow thing trying to get in my room."

Grandma suddenly turned and sat up straighter, "Child, tell me everything. Don't leave out one detail." I was more than happy to let her have it. I didn't leave out one emotion, feeling or thought. I finished and let out a sigh of relief, like getting it said made it better somehow. Even though grandma had a serious look, she had a sort of smirky grin as we stood up to start walking.

"Child, you have been greatly honored. First by Satan and then by Jesus." "Honored? Are you kidding me? You're going to have to help me with that stretch. It sure doesn't feel like an honor to me." Grandma chuckled, "We're going to cover a lot of bible today and even though you have read it, you'll soon develop a hunger for reading it. Yes child, honored.

Do you know that the word 'Satan' is a Hebrew word?" She didn't have to wait for an answer but she did, "No Ma'am." She continued, "It is and the definition is opponent or adversary." She reached into her coat pocket and pulled out a small leather-bound Bible. The leather was worn and chipped around the edges but you could easily see that it was very old. The leather on it was way thicker than anything I had seen on today's books. "This was my grandmother's Bible. It is the only one I have ever had.

Look here, Ephesians 6:11-12 Put on the whole armor of God, that ye may be able to stand against the wiles of the devil. For we wrestle not against flesh and blood, but against principalities, against powers, against the rulers of the darkness of this world, against spiritual wickedness in high places. You see that word I have underlined, 'wiles'?" "Yes Ma'am."

She closed the Bible and began, "The definition of that word is, 'trickery in perception'. Since you have died to self and currently do not have a focal point or a new direction in life, it would be the perfect time for him to try to induce fear. But what he has really done is brought you great honor."

I shook my head, "Grandma, please, no riddles. Explain this to me in such a way that I can understand." She seemed more excited about this than anything so far. "Child, The Bible shows us specific character attributes and habits of the devil. If you were to study a person, you would make a list of the things they did and maybe a list of things they didn't do that maybe they should have. Let's look at the Shadow Man."

We sat down on the nearest bench and she opened her Bible. "Satan operates the same way every time. In the garden with Eve he tricked her perception in three areas, lust of the flesh, lust of the eye and the pride of life. We see his first tactic is to talk behind someone's back. When you meet someone, who talks about others then you are seeing and adversary. Satan would not have said those things to Eve had God been standing there.

In the wilderness he tempted Jesus with lust of the flesh with bread, lust of the eye with riches and the pride of life with casting himself off the temple so everyone would know he was the Son of God. But Jesus had a purpose, a focal point so he did not come to satisfy the flesh, nor to be satisfied by wealth or even to be worshipped or adored.

Jesus taught us the parable of the sower and in it he said, as soon as the word was sown, the devil comes and tries to steal the word from your heart. This is part of what he came to your room for. To make himself the center of your focus and by doing so, taking your focus and energy off-of your purpose.

Then, in the garden Satan was after Eve's seed, or what we would say, after her children." This is also what he came for, to steal your seed, your children of faith. If he stops you by tricking your perception or changing your focus, then he effectively eliminates you as a sower of the seeds of faith.

Child, you are a threat to him or he would not have shown up, himself. It is, actually a great honor to have disturbed him. Secondly, Jesus called you up and gave you a call to minister. 'Go. Get what is Mine!', The prayers belong to him but the Demon of Doubt steals them right off the alter of God because Satan has altered their perception of self-worth.

He came for you but since he couldn't get you he will come to divert your seed, if he can't do that he'll come for the diaries. You will fight him all your days. You will always win but a fight it will be. The Bible tells us to fight the good fight of faith. Maybe not in your life but you will fight him by proxy, in the life of your children of faith."

I thought about things she said and tried to put my questions in the order in which she said them. "Grandma, I see what you mean about trickery in perception being the wiles of the devil and I see that this trickery will always be in the soul, the mind or the emotions by changing a person's focal point. That is, really good.

I can see how that works in everyday life and business but you called him the demon of doubt. Mind explaining?" "Sure", she said, "Grandpa and I were at a church service once where a young preacher was praying for the sick. A grandmother brought up a young girl without hair, to be prayed for. It was cancer and the sight of the girl humbled the preacher to tears. For some reason he felt he could not pray for the child so he asked anyone who felt lead by the Lord to pray for this child, to come up. Brigit Fayth was about twelve at the time and she darted out and went up and laid hands on the child.

On the way home, grandpa ask her why she felt lead to pray, she said, 'I knew I might be the only one there that would not let the demon of doubt steal my prayer.'. Ever since then, the shadow man has always been called the demon of doubt around here."

I picked up on what she said, "Grandma, three things, did grandma Fayth have the same dream that I did? Second, it sounds like he has been here before and why couldn't he get in my room, the door was unlocked?" She stood up and I followed. "Not the same dream but she had several encounters with the thief. The Bible says, 'The thief came to steal, kill and destroy', and yes, he always stops by to test our new students.

Now, why couldn't he get in? That's simple, the innocent blood of the Lamb of God. Satan cannot cross the threshold of innocent blood. South Gate is the house that faith built and we are in covenant with Jesus." We stopped by the Moringa Tree, "I remember Grandma Grace's preacher explaining the blood covenant so I understand that, but after the diaries?" Grandma's face became real stern.

"Child, he has been after those diaries from the day we got them. We have kept them protected by the blood every day. They have never been outside the blood line. The diaries, contain power to transform everyone, who comes in to contact with them. You will receive them and learn them and then as darkness begins, there will become a hunger and thirst in the spirit that only those diaries can quench. The valley of dry bones the Bible calls it.

They are in order and you must absorb and assimilate each one before moving to the next. There is an extreme danger if the Demon of Doubt steals one or more of the diaries. The order of the doctrines must be maintained or spiritual abnormalities will result in your children of faith and alter the outcomes for America and the Church for over two thousand years.

Women have carried these truths through the ages and Lydia, the seller of purple is responsible for most all of Paul's letters. She unlocked Asia Minor and the Bible we have ends with the book of Revelations which is an address to the seven churches in Asia Minor. Paul did a lot of talking, but Lydia did a lot of doing. She was a business woman and had an extremely strong self-image and self-will. She spent all her life and money acquiring the diaries. Child, let me say this, any one of the diaries is worth it all. Lydia's is the first diary and when I read it, I became stronger that very day than I had ever been in my entire life.

Your spirit is like a small infant child, it feeds on the illumination from the Father of Spirits. Each diary is an explosion of light and you grow exponentially each day. Okay child, we have covered many things over the past three days but the most important thing I must teach you is worship."

My mind quickly imagined people singing in the choir and holy rollers running through the aisles. "What exactly do you mean?" Grandma smiled and picked a few seed tops from a low growing plant, "Do you know what worship is?" I answered as she handed me a couple, "It brings to mind, what I saw on TV that they call praise and worship. A bunch of people singing, shouting and some running."

Grandma tosses a couple of seed tops in her mouth and told me to try them. I was hesitant but I did. "That is sweet. What is it?" "Red Clover. Makes the best honey if you have some bees nearby. Deer love it too. They come out on the side of the roads to eat it." I remembered the deer in the road on my trip down, as she continued.

"I'm not talking about what you do toward Jesus, that is praise and you get to do that throughout eternity. I am talking about what you do for him. Most people refuse to worship." I swallowed the seeds, "For him? I don't see what you mean." Grandma turned toward me, "External locus of control verses internal locus of control."

I must have looked puzzled as she continued. "Let's look at your life up until now. Your success always depended on another job, better education or the right people. If you met the right people or was at the right place, then you got the right success. That is completely being controlled by the external. Just like many that praise our Lord. They need to feel something or experience something in order to satisfy the mind or emotions.

But worship is a verb, not a noun. In Bible times, worship was done by bringing something to the temple. Today, worship is what you do for him, not toward him. It is an internal locus of control. An internal drive to do something for Jesus. In olden times it was a lamb without spot or blemish, today it is your labor, done without a spot of self-motive or blemished by self-aggrandizement."

I seemed to recognize where this was going. Buy now, I was regaining my sense of projected listening and knew she was laying the groundwork to connect my focus and energy toward some greater good.

"Grandma, before we refocus my priorities, can you give me one good reason why I need to do this?" "Child, I'll give you three.

First, the Bible says, 'He that knoweth to do good and doeth it not, to him that is sin.'.

Second, one split second after you close your eyes in death to this world, you will open your eyes in one of two placed. A place of light and love or complete darkness and fear. You can choose love or you can choose self, but you will choose one.

No one goes to Heaven that doesn't choose to.

You can choose a place of eternal light and love or darkness. A darkness so dark that the Bible says a candle cannot light it. The shadow man's domain.

And finally, the third reason, the children of faith. Without the Ark of Faith, they will perish, just as they did in the floods of Noah, with a mother holding up her famine stricken child before her own health fails. The pictures of those sufferings will haunt you throughout eternity because God has chosen you."

I swallowed hard as the graphic images of famine stricken countries seem to cover the American land like dust settling from a tornado. "Grandma, what do I do and how do I do it?"

Grandma hugged me and I knew it meant goodbye. I could feel tears swelling up inside and as she stepped back, she too had tears. "Grandma, I didn't think angels could cry?" "Child, grandpa will teach you the disciplines. Leaving you now is harder than all the years waiting for you but the Lord says my job is though. After you learn from the diaries, you must release them like a flock of doves. Do not hide them under a stone as we have had to do."

She turned and walked slowly and reluctantly down the long center aisle. I watched her every move, her laced boots as they touched the dirt floor, her distinguished style with her ranch coat and her hair scarf. She turned right and disappeared behind the plants. I stared for a long while, looking at every inch of the greenhouse, thinking of the hours and hours she must have spent there, teaching others the ways of God.

How her worship shouted at me from every plant and bench and walkway. I thought about how much I had learned in such a short time with her. Part of me felt deathly alone, a type of alone that I had never felt, but the plant's praises rose up like thunder from a valley floor, echoing the coming of a storm. A storm so great that God opened-up the envelope of time and bridged four generations to send the keys to the Ark of Heaven.

Chapter Nine

Midday Christmas Eve

My legs seemed to be stuck, like learning to walk again. I slowly followed grandmothers path and turned right at the end of the aisle. I thought of what she had said about the diaries, how they hid them under a stone and when she said they had never been outside the blood line so they would be protected from the shadow man.

Outside the greenhouse, the sun was bright but much cooler air had set in. It was beginning to feel more like the winter I was accustomed to. I made it up the back steps on to the deck and entered the kitchen. Everyone was there, bright eyed and silent, just waiting on me to share.

"Want something to eat, Mrs. Lydia?", Elizabeth inquired. "Yes, please" as I made my way around the breakfast bar where Kevin and Ryan were sitting. I proceeded to catch them up on all the things I had learned and the questions that it naturally raised.

"Ryan, you were quiet while I told everyone what Grandpa taught me and about the round calendar. What are your thoughts on the seasons and grandpa's tapestry of time?" Ryan turned his chair a little, which made it appear his response may take a while.

"Mrs. Lydia, I have never studied the fixed stars to any large degree. But what you have told me has shown me how Manoah was able to be so accurate with times and events. Most us country folk know the Sun and moon very well. But very few know anything about the eight other time pieces or the twelve thresholds. When you bring in the fixed stars, you are way out of our league.

When you bring in Father Time crossing into darkness, that means Saturn will be crossing the ascendant line and entering the seven and one quarter years of fall, followed by seven and one quarter years of winter. So, I can see what he is saying about the season but the four horsemen of Revelations?

Wow! The fixed stars move one degree every sixty years, so for the Red Horse to be on the ascendant line in America's birth chart at the very moment that Satan and the Sun arrive, it will take 2160 years for the Red Horse to be back in the same place but Satan and the Sun would not be because their differing orbit times.

Mrs. Lydia, the odds of accuracy of Manoah's circular calendar is 2160, times 12 houses, times 365 days, times 24 hours, times 60 minutes, to one. For him to give you an exact time on an exact day, and then, be able to explain his conclusion is so far beyond me, I really do not have any doubt.

As soon as I see the diaries in your hands tomorrow, I am headed straight home and calling an emergency church meeting to inform them of the dangers ahead. Everyone around here has grown up hearing about Manoah, so when I share his conclusion, this town will burst into action. Country folk have always been a covenant people."

Kevin and Katrina looked back toward Elizabeth who had begun washing a few dished. Katrina asked, "Mrs. Elizabeth, this sounds real serious. Are you worried?" "Nope. Not in the least." she replied. Kevin spoke up, "Don't you believe it?" "Elizabeth turned toward them, "Every bit of it! I sure do. But worry, not on your life. God is not leaving South Gate and neither am I. Trust in the Lord and lean not on to your own understanding, but in all your ways acknowledge him and he will direct your path. I am doing exactly what he has called me to do and I fully intend to continue to do so. It is what I was made for and what I truly love."

Kevin looked at Ryan, "We can handle our food supplies but what's after that?" Ryan looked back toward me, "Mrs. Lydia, I am a forth, generation preacher. During all my time growing up, Dad and Granddad always talked about how troubled times brought out the best and worst in people. Most folks are going to walk directly into the eye of this storm, never knowing it was coming. How do I answer questions like Kevin's?"

I just stared at him for a moment, "I really don't know yet. I get the feeling that Grandpa will complete my training for something but, the questions arise from a sense of security or self-defense. I get the feeling that Grandma and Grandpa are teaching me offense. I believe we are about to move forward, not backwards."

The room got quiet, Ryan was grinning and Elizabeth had stopped washing and stood looking at me, with her hand on her hip. "Mrs. Lydia, you are starting to sound like your Grandmother Fayth. The devil could serve her rotten food and she would make compost. She always said, 'Don't respond to ignorance. Ignorance is compounded by comment. The only Christians who gets second best are those that accept it.'"

Everyone smiled or chuckled and I thought about Grandma Fayth. I wondered how she was doing and if she had come home from the hospital. "Elizabeth, would you call to see how she is doing? Last time I saw her see was making me leave the hospital room so I could arrive here on time."

"Absolutely. Will do that right now but she was doing fine yesterday but was still there. I've had to keep her updated or she had threatened to leave.", Elizabeth responded and walked toward the great room.

"Ryan. Can you meet me here a couple of hours before dark? I have some bible questions I need to work through before I meet Grandpa this evening." Kevin and Katrina interjected quickly, "Can we come?" I smiled, "Oh yes. Please do." Kevin looked at Ryan, "I'll get out the white boards!" Ryan smiled extremely big and with his best country boy charm looked at me and said, "Just remember, you asked for it."

I laughed and told them all I would see them in a few hours and went to my room to rest, and to ponder the question, 'What is winning?'. After a long shower, I laid across the bed asking myself over and over, 'What is winning? Who is winning? How to win and what does one get who wins? I must have slept for a few hours but woke to the sound of Elizabeth knocking at my door. "Mrs. Lydia, are you awake? Ryan is down stairs."

I felt refreshed, just like a full night sleep and told her I'd be down in just a minute. Down stairs Ryan, Kevin and Katrina were all in the great room and had three white boards already on stands and a bunch of books on the table in front of the couches. Ryan began, "Mrs. Lydia, after we spoke today, I called my Dad and Granddad. I believe we have a hundred questions for Manoah but I told them that Manoah has been sent to equip you to fulfill God's plan and that we would be able

164

to get our answers from you in a few days, after you had a chance to study the diaries. I hope that answer was okay?"

I smiled, "Ryan, all I can say is that I will do my best." "Granddad said Manoah and Margaret dedicated their lives to doing the Lord's work and never faltered. He also said that both Grace and Fayth had to make the same choice with their lives and worked to doing the Lord's work all their days. That is the sole reason South Gate is here today. He prayed that you would find that strength also. He said that giving up your own priorities to do the Lord's work was the hardest decision you would ever make. Dad added that it was never an easy thing when the self, dies, when you set your priorities aside and pick up Christ's."

Their words struck me. I thought for a moment and dying to self finally came to light. I had always thought dying to self was some spiritual out of body experience of some kind. "Ryan, tell your Dad and Granddad that they may never know how much their words have helped me tonight."

I made my way to the couch and examined the books with a quick glance. Katrina bounced down beside me like she was my little sister while Kevin stood just off her side of the couch. Elizabeth took her seat in what appeared to be her recliner and Ryan grabbed a marker and went toward the boards.

I said, "Correct me if I'm wrong but it appears that all of you have done this before." The room broke into laughter, "Mrs. Lydia, we do this every Wednesday night from seven to whenever. Normally there are forty plus people here. Thirty students and other family members.", Elizabeth said with a great big smile. Kevin ask Ryan to open in prayer. Ryan looked

165

toward the ceiling and started, "Lord, where two or more are gathered in your name, you are in the midst thereof. We come together tonight to assist Mrs. Lydia and seek your will and knowledge. You said the Holy Ghost would guide us into all truth and that is what we are here to receive. Amen.

Now Mrs. Lydia, we have less than two hours before dark, what questions do we need to examine?" I thought for a few seconds and simply asked, "Explain what winning is. Give me the who, what, when, where, why and how of winning as it pertains to this South Gate event and the prophecy of dark times."

Ryan was surprisingly methodical as he wrote the six words down the left side of the board. "Some of these I can answer quickly. Who is winning and what they are winning? The winners are, you, me, everyone in this room and everyone who hears the prophecy. What are they winning?" He wrote down each winner across the top of the board, "You win super big. Do you know anyone else that has got a call on their life and God sent their great, great, great grandparents back to teach them for three days? Do you know how many people in history that have held the diaries from the women in the upper room? Do you care to guess the value of their content? And not least is the fact that many rewards are still to come. I win from the knowledge shared. My family wins because we can now prepare for dark times. The same goes for everyone here and especially all those that you reach and teach will win big.

Now, let's carry this one step further, what are we losing? Me, nothing. Everyone else that receives your teachings, nothing. Those that don't hear you or don't believe you, might lose it all, including their lives. You, on the other hand, let's examine. Are you losing your job?" I shook my head. "Are you losing any of your possessions?" Again, I shook my head. "Are you losing your family?" I hesitated for a moment as I thought about Robert. It wasn't caused by this so I shook my head no. "That pretty much covers all the who's and what."

I dropped in a thought, "I am losing my life, my goals and agenda." There was a short silence. Ryan looked toward the ceiling again. "I'm not so sure. Are you? I mean, are not your goals and dreams compatible with your calling? If you're not losing your job, possessions or family, then how do you perceive that your losing your goals and dreams?"

The word, 'perceive' went off like a morning alarm clock in my head. Trickeries in perception was what Grandma called it. Ryan waited and when I didn't respond he continued, "Now, I think when and where are self-explanatory. Why? That is easy, the Bible says, 'God is Love'. The reason we are all winning is because God loves." Elizabeth jumped in, "For God so loved the world". Katrina finished the verse, "that he gave his only begotten son, that whosoever believed in him should not perish but have everlasting life.". Kevin joined in as well, "Romans says that nothing can separate us from the love of God."

Ryan went to another white board, "Let's look at 'How to win'?'. As best as I can figure, Manoah, has to give you this answer tonight. I can see how to win in bits and pieces but to effect outcomes hundreds and even thousands of years forward, we are missing a big portion of understanding."

I sat and stared at the boards. Why couldn't I reason this out, upstairs? I am a human calculator. I can evaluate the most complex issues in quantum algebra, zero sum games and interactive decision theory. I understand decision science better than any president or politician alive and love still makes no sense. It has no why, no integer value, is divisible and yet loses no value. Robert laughs at me and says I can't figure it out because it is real but intangible. He says that love is a sum-game. The more you divide it, the greater it becomes.

"Ryan, love does not compute in decision science. The basis for all decisions, with animals or humans, are based on reward, pain or pleasure. All knowledge is based on a comparison, good defines evil, high defines low and so on. And decisions between two or more parties can be placed on a balance beam and the objective is equilibrium or zero sum. I have studied heterodox economics and circular theory and even though Grandpa asked me to give him and Grandma three days before I allowed my binary reasoning to kick in, please show me how God wins, man wins, God loses and man loses.

He is a player in this cooperative and non-cooperative game theory. Some people are cooperative and others will be non-cooperative in this game matrix. The term, 'Game Changer' comes from the study of Game Theory and is when someone or something changes a rule or set of rules in the game, thusly changing all outcomes. Some rule by Chaos and effectively function by the Game Changer Strategies. You will see this played out when a president and administration sets up new rules in any number of divisions to alter the game in their favor.

Now, God has set the rules and parameters for the events on earth and I am a cooperative member. Please explain to me God's net sum gain." Ryan walked slowly to the third white board. He took a red marker from the box on the table and drew a very big heart. Turned toward me with a gentle look, "Lydia, most of what you said, I have no idea what you are talking about. It sounds like you are highly educated and I respect that. I do believe I get the idea of your question and I think I can answer it, if you will let me?"

I assumed Ryan thought I was mad but I really wasn't. "Please do. It is a sincere question." Ryan turned back toward the board, "Mrs. Lydia, you can be smart, all by yourself. You can be wealthy, all by yourself. You can be creative, all by yourself. But the one thing you cannot do alone is love. God was creative, all by himself. He is all knowing, all by himself. He is wealthy, all by himself. But he could not love, have friendship or fellowship alone, so he created man to have friendship, fellowship and love.

He created a perfect garden planet for his man to dwell in and gave man the authority over it, the lease agreement. But man became self-aware and soon fell into self-centeredness. Man became his own god and set up his own rules and began to dominate other men, then fellowship and love was lost. God wins love and fellowship and that will be hard for you to place a value on."

I was taken back by his gentle response. The last debate we had, he was forceful. "Fair enough", I said. He continued, "Since you like to evaluate decisions, there is a story in the Bible that I would like to share and get your thoughts.

You know the story of David, the one who killed Goliath?" I nodded. "God told the prophet to go to the house of Jesse and anoint one of his son king. The prophet arrived and Jesse paraded seven sons by him but God did not quicken the prophet on any. He asked the father if he had any other sons. Jesse responded that he had only one small boy watching sheep.

169

Upon arriving, David was anointed. It would be natural to think that David should rise to fame, God had chosen him. But David had to fight a lion and then a bear and then Goliath. He was given wealth and the kings daughter in marriage, but the king turned on him.

Later in years he still wanted to do good for God and returned the Ark of God to Jerusalem. He danced in front of the parade, he was so happy. That evening, he went into his wife and she said that he had made a fool of himself.

Lydia, we turn just a page and we find David in the bed with another woman. Care to analyze why?" I thought back to my first encounter with Ryan and how I thought about his innocent smile. I should have slapped him for picking me up and sitting me on the tailgate.

"He did not get the reward from his wife and pursued reward elsewhere." Ryan seemed to be heading somewhere with this, so I waited.

"Mrs. Lydia, the Bible teaches us that man looks on the outward conduct of man but God looks on the inward decision-making parts.

You see, David was rejected by his father and the spirit of rejection never left him. Then the king rejected him and finally his wife rejected him. Then we find him trying to fill the void of rejection with a woman. Some people fight all their lives against the spirit of lust, but if you heal the spirit of rejection, lust will leave."

I thought for a moment, "What does this have to do with me or God winning?" Ryan was drawing on the red heart and was carefully measuring his response, "The spirit of rejection is a crafty devil, it's funny how he can make a person think their father didn't love them. Sometimes it's true, sometimes not and sometimes he just had to work and was never there. But that person will always set up defense shields against the pain of losing love and at the same time will find a pleasure or reward type behavior to make themselves feel worthy of admiration.

Whether they fill the wound with sex or achievements. Mrs. Lydia, love is not a calculated response with a measurable reward. If it were, a fireman would never rush into a burning building to save a child." I realized Ryan didn't know anything about my father but I think he just nailed my psyche to the white board.

I plotted my escape, "That helps me a lot. I think it's about time for me to get my questions ready for tonight." I excused myself and drug my inner self up the stairs, bumping her head on every step. At the top of the stairs I stopped and looked back, funny how steps look different from the top.

Chapter Ten

Grandpa's Last Night

I sat on my bed until darkness filled the room. I listened to every sound of the night as I hoped to catch the sound of grandpa on the balcony. Somehow, I just seemed to notice the sound of a rocker easing back and forth. I picked up my jacket at the foot of the bed as I made my way to the balcony doors.

Grandpa smiled as I came out, "Mrs. Lydia Fayth. You were expecting me." I smiled back, "As Grandma said on my first encounter, 'I wasn't expecting a substitute teacher.'" We both laughed and I took my seat. "Well child, have any questions for me on this lovely Christmas Eve night?"

I looked at him for a few seconds and then just shook my head no. We sat looking at the round calendar and the Angels for a little while and just rocked back and forth like a grandfather and granddaughter would after a hard day's work.

I thought about what Ryan had said and how my father was never around. I thought about how the Spirit of Rejection would motivate differing conducts and how I snapped at Robert before I left. I looked at Grandpa and wondered why I had not rejected his male character like I apparently did with most all males.

"Grandpa, what is the Spirit of Rejection?", I asked as if it were a passing thought. He didn't change the mood but as he rocked, he answered with a, matter of fact gentleness, "An outward sign of an inward condition." I tried to analysis what he meant but I was becoming accustomed to riddles, "Care to draw this math major a picture?"

He found my reply humorous, "Sure will. If a person fills their mind and emotions with hate, hate will pour out. If a person fills their mind and emotions with self-pity, that is what will come out. If a person's mind and emotions feel rejection for an extended period, their response to rejection will come out. So, the inward conditioning of a person's spirit will demonstrate outward signs of that condition."

My mind raced to apply this reasoning to my father. "So, if dad worked all the time and it was just me and mom most of my young life then, over a prolong period of time, it is possible that I associated dad's absence to him rejecting me?"

The subject didn't seem to bother him, "Much worse than that, you would have also associated him as rejecting your mother. It would be a natural response for you to also see yourself defending your mother from rejection. The first would be an internal defense but the latter could take on the form of aggressive defense.

Are you having difficulties with dominate males?" I could feel my blood pressure rising as the subject wasn't comfortable. "It has crossed my mind." I was thinking how I really shouldn't have brought this up.

"Well child, becoming aware of it is curative. Once it is illuminated to you, you have the control over it. Imagine that you have a picture of your dad in a large frame but the glass has a smoky glaze on it. You washed and washed the glass but could not get the glaze clean. In your mind, take down the picture, take a hammer then strike the glass and break it into pieces. Now look at your dad. You can see him smiling at you as clean and clear as a winter sunshine."

I thought on what he said for a few minutes as we continued to rock. He broke the silence, "Sure there isn't any questions?" I couldn't help but respond, "My mind is going in two or three directions at once. One part of me is examining the effects of rejection and how I told my husband to leave.

Another part is trying to figure out what God wants and what winning is and the other part is trying to re-establish direction in life. This is our last evening and I still do not know what to do."

He seemed to rock a little faster as he responded, "Now that gives me something to work with. Can I help answer those for you?" I nodded yes. "Well then, let's take it one part at a time. If the Spirit of Rejection is not expelled from your life, then pretty, soon, what the Bible calls, the Spirit of infirmity will also infect your spirit." I thought about what Grandma taught me with the three rings of healing. "Grandma drew me a picture of the three rings and you taught me about the trichotomy."

He grinned business like, "Many women wrestle, with the Spirit of Rejection and often-times it leads to the Spirit of Infirmity. I think your doctors call it 'Learned Helplessness' and then depression but then it moves on the auto-immune system. The Bible says it is anything that causes insecurity or unstableness.

The real question is, 'Do you love your husband?'" I thought for a minute, "What is love? It is hard to define and definitely cannot be calculated." He smiled as he began, "Well, for a thinking person like yourself, I need to break it down. There are many types of love and they are measured, many different ways.

First there is Philia which is a deep, non-sexual friendship between close friends, family members or a deep bond of friendship by soldiers as they fought alongside each other in battle.

Pragma is the mature love that develops over a long period of time between long-term couples and develops by shared values.

Agape is a more generalized love, it's about love for all of humanity.

Philautia is self-love, how you value yourself will determine how you care for others.

Last there is Eros, it is about sexual passion and desire. Unless it grows into Pragma, it will burn itself out. Many relationships are founded upon this one and that is why they end so often.

The values based relationships are the ones that stand the test of time and you can easily calculate these. The Bible says that two cannot walk together unless they are joined and that joining is in values.

Let's look at the Spirit of Divorce. As with any relationship, if every time you communicate with them there is negative emotions or problems discussed, then pretty soon you do not want to see them. You see his face, you perceive a problem, you see his face, you hear negative, you see his face, you argue. It will not be long before you do not want to see his face, thus you have the spirit of divorce because of compounding negatives.

If you have developed a shield due to your father, then that shield may prohibit you from seeing your husband's true values.

Now let's look at your internal definition of love. Most people believe that success in love depends on meeting some magical soul mate and somewhere out there in the world, the forces of destiny are going to fling them together. Now these very same people believe that business success is based on hard work and effort. But when it comes to love they assume that if this is the perfect person then it would require no effort. But when effort is required, they say to themselves that this can't be the right person for me. No other area of life works in this manner and that is why there is so much divorce.

There are only two real question that need to be answered. Do you want to succeed in marriage the same way as other areas of life and do you and he share common values?"

I sat there feeling like he just pulled out my brain and wrung it out like a dishrag. Grandpa must have noticed, "My child, do you want to be successful in your partnership with him and do you and he share similar values?" I looked directly into grandpa's eyes. He was sincere. He wasn't trying to maneuver me. "I always want to succeed. Failure is the wrong color for me, I don't wear it well. Robert and I do share a common set of value. He loves me and I love me," grandpa laughed, "but I really don't think I have that value anymore. It's not that I value myself any less, it's just that the priorities of my values have completely shifted. I don't think that I am the most important issue, given the coming storm. Robert always puts others first and given what you, Grandma and the Lord have shown me, I can't think of anyone on earth I would want on my side more than him and my family."

Grandpa just kept rocking, "Mrs. Lydia Fayth, I believe you have some pretty good clout with the Lord. I'm pretty sure if you asked him for something, he'd more than likely make sure you got it." I smiled but this was more serious than that, "Grandpa, what should I do first?"

"Repent is where I always started.", he said. That word caught me off guard, "Repent? That sounds ugly." He smiled, "The word means change directions. Lot of folk have a bunch of emotion tied to that word that really don't have to. If I were on a train carrying me in the wrong direction, the moment I realized it, I would get off and catch the next train headed in the direction I wanted to go. Changing direction is just that simple.

Is your marriage going in the direction you want?" I shook my head as I answered, "No." "Then I'll wait here while you step in and call him." I thought for a minute, "Grandpa, I'll call him after my time with you."

Grandpa stopped rocking, "Never ever wait to repent. Lydia, all of heaven stops when someone repents. I'll wait." I felt a lump rising in my throat and tears welling up. I step inside and went to my phone beside the bed. The phone rang and I realized I was trembling. It rang a second time and I had to set down on the bed, Robert answered in mid ring. "Yes, my beautiful lady, I have garnished you a lovely tree and all our shopping is done. When are you coming home? Santa has arrived and I bet you are going to be surprise."

I could sense his jubilant cover, and I tried to control my

quivering voice, "Robert, I am so sorry. I have learned so much and I don't want you to leave." I lost it. It was like a river of hate and rejection just seem to break over the damn and I had no way to contain it. I began to cry uncontrollably, "Please wait for me. I'll be a couple of days but I'm coming home and I need you." Robert didn't speak for a few seconds, "Lydia, what's wrong? Do you need me to come, get you?" I could sense his alarm. He had never seen me or heard me in a state that I was not in total control. "Baby, just hold on, I'll have the police there in a minute and I'm on my way." Robert, you don't understand. I'm fine. I just have learned so much. The letter was all true. I have so much to share with you. Just wait for me." I could only imagine his shock but the night would not last forever. "Robert, I have to go but I'll call you in the morning. I love you." He was still not assured, Lydia baby, you're not sounding right. Are you sure you're alright?" I knew there was only one way to convince him that I hadn't lost my mind or had been kidnapped, "I'm perfectly fine but I'm not your baby. I'm your wife."

He hesitated just a second, "Oh. I thought I lost you there for a minute. Baby, I love you and I'll be here." We said our goodbyes for the night and I returned to the balcony to find Grandpa standing by the rail, looking at the calendar.

"Why does it feel like I was holding on to the spirit of rejection and it was not holding on to me? I mean, the moment I let go, it left." Grandpa didn't look at me but answered, "No one can enter a strongman's house, unless he first binds the strongman. Once an evil spirit is cast out, he looks to and fro to find a dwelling place. Finding none he returns to his house. If it is not occupied by a stronger spirit, he will again abide.

179

Love entered your spirit and the destructive spirit had to leave, so you did not have to fight the spirit, Love did. That is why it felt like letting go. All you had to do was open up the door. When the Holy Spirit enters, all that is needed is illumination in each room, or area of your life."

I thought about how deep every sentence he spoke seemed to be. "Grandpa, I'm lost. If I am steering the Ark of Faith, it is a ship in the sea of time and I do not have a map to my destination, then I am lost at sea." He turned his head with a peculiar look, "Parables suit you. Your choice of words, align well with our lesson, last night, on faith mapping and all knowledge is for navigation. Well done." He turned to go down the steps and I followed.

"Lydia, let's get down to business. Are you ready to worship the Lord?" I thought about Grandma and her definition of worship. "I am ready to do want I can." He stopped in mid step, "Stop thinking about yourself! Are you ready to worship or not?" I didn't know what to say. He continued with a softer tone, "The first night you use five 'I' s in your sentence. Tonight, you used two. It is simply, I am or no."

I didn't feel like I was being corrected or even being spoke down to but I quickly responded, "I am." He turned and continued walking to the round calendar. "We have to cover a tremendous amount tonight and it will all be short and in outline type form.

The diaries will guide you but tonight the Lord will give to you, instructions after I leave. What did the Lord tell you last night?" We sat down in the garden and I shared the entire vision and dream. "He told you to go get what was his?" "Yes sir. That is what he said." I waited on his response.

"Okay then, what was his?" "The prayers", I said. He shook his head, "No ma'am. The Glory is his! Yes, the prayers belong to him but it is not the prayer that glorifies the Father, it is the answer! The Glory is the outshining! If that grandmother was healed by the love of God, that my dear Lydia, is the Shekinah Glory of God. The outshining of God.

That is what the demon of doubt robbed from the alter and the children of God." I smiled at the thought of the sick grandmother slapping the shadow man as he came near her bed.

"Grandpa, isn't the church doing this already?" Grandpa's face became sad, "The church is the body of Christ and Christ is the Bread of Life. Every place in scripture where Jesus was given bread, he took the bread, he broke the bread and he gave it to the disciples to serve the bread.

This time of darkness is when he breaks the bread. The breaking of the church, the breaking of the body. You have been seeing this division growing and growing over the last few years. The church is divided by doctrines they created and even the pope quit. How many children have been lost? They are more concerned with their commerce than the Lord's children.

Tithing always had a two-way flow. Into the covenant body and back to the needs of the covenant family. Now you can tithe for twenty years but don't ever get sick or homeless. Don't ever find yourself in need. The church will dump you like a cloud dumps rain.

They are verifiable strangers to the word and doctrine of covenant. And strangers to the character and nature of Christ, the God they claim to be in covenant with. If they claim to be in covenant with a man that healed the sick, feed the hungry and illuminated truth from house to house, then it would follow to reason that you should see them doing that from time to time.

But, that is why you were preordained four generations ago, you are the disciple he is giving the Bread of Life to serve his children." I thought of a few scandals I read about in the news. It wasn't hard to see divisions in the church.

"Grandpa, what does God want? I mean, what is winning for him?" Grandpa began to pace back and forth a few steps away, "Lydia, God wants fellowship with his creation. Winning to God is getting his children back. His desire is to speak with them the way he has been speaking to you and much, much more shall you fellowship with him as you walk out your days.

He walked with them in the garden, he provided for them, he created for them. Then his adversary destroyed the relationship." I guess I was having a 'Thomas Payne' moment of logical questioning,

"Grandpa, I don't see what you mean." He stopped for a moment and stared into the night sky. He looked back at me, "Let's sit for a moment. Have you ever read where Moses saw the goodness of God and his face glowed so bright that the people had him were a veil?" I smiled, "Yes sir."

He continued, "In the garden, Adam and Eve walked with God. They could not see their nakedness because their entire body glowed. But we read in Isaiah that the Arch Angel Lucifer saw his own beauty, became self-aware and decided to exalt himself above God, thus becoming God's adversary, Satan. The Hebrew word for adversary is Satan. God cast him out of the heavens and we find him in the garden. He convinced Eve to take of the tree of binary thought, the tree of the knowledge of good and evil. But unknown to her was that disobedience would make their bodies lose the light of righteousness. She ate and gave to Adam and he ate and they saw their nakedness, their glow was gone. They became, 'self-aware.

The same condition that Lucifer had, he infected man with. Before this, man walked with God spirit to spirit but because of Satan, the soul of man was enthroned.

Now, place yourself in God's position. You leave your children in the kitchen and your one law is to not eat from the poison tree. When you return, you can't find them, the tree has been eaten up. Now, any loving parent would search frantically to find their children.

But sin is a condition in the spirit. The condition of 'Self Intending Nature' is not something you can just take a pill for. Remember, they can see themselves, they do not glow anymore. Now everything is compared to them, their feelings and their mind. They and all the children of the earth have this condition and you hear things like, 'I think God is this, I believe God is that' and sometime 'I believe God understands, he made us this way'."

I sat there and just stared, there wasn't any way I could believe man made the earth, this beautiful palace and no way could he make himself. If God created the palace planet and created man then I could see fallen man and for the first time, I could understand the love of God as a father.

"Grandpa, how do I help?" You could sense a greater energy coming from him as he realized our time was short and we were moving toward something more concrete. "Lydia, returning the children to God is not that easy but Jesus gave us a pattern. The diaries will carry you step by step and your understanding will be illuminated. I have made chapter and verse notes in each diary to help you study. The diaries were written before the bible so you may need to cross reference.

They must be born of the spirit to walk with God. Faith is the birth canal and your job is to teach people to be Faith Coaches. You will sow the seeds of God. Anyone who comes to God must believe that he is and that he is a rewarder of them that seek him.

The first diary is from Lydia, the seller of purple. She will teach you how to show them, trust in a living God. Each diary after that will equip you to fulfill his charge, 'Go get what is mine'.

Tonight, the Lord will illuminate your next steps and tomorrow you will receive the diaries." He stood up and I knew our time had run out, "Grandpa, can I ever see you and Grandma again? I mean, here?" "Child, we will be watching you every day. Your dad and all the heavenly host will rejoice at every child you reach, every parent you teach and every teacher you equip. But you must walk with the Lord and if you walk in the spirit, you will have fellowship with us all. Just call and you will sense our presence.

But my job is done." "Grandpa, how will I get the diaries and where should I keep them?" He started turning away but stopped briefly, "The fragrance of Christ shall guide you." He finished turning and I watched him disappear into the darkened tree line just past the greenhouse. A chill sweep over me like a passing breeze. I looked toward the sky and watched a dark cloud hide the light of the moon. All the angel's shadows were gone and the calendar was dark. My mine raced at the thought of dark times.

I looked at the house and saw the solar lights sparkling along the walkway. I thought how following God was like moving toward one light at a time and how some day following those lights would lead to the doors of his throne room.

I made it to my room and knelt to pray, "God, I want to help. Please show me what to do. Know my thankfulness tonight is greater than I can express. Amen" I turned back the covers and laid there thinking about diaries, devils, darkness and my Robert. There is something indescribable about knowing you have a real friend and partner.

The Third Dream

I woke as water was splashed on my face. I looked around and the people were all standing alongside a river. I was standing in knee deep water and beside me, a bearded man just had raise a teenage girl up from the river. He looked at me and spoke, "Do you baptize in this river?" I was at a loss for an answer, "Sir, I don't baptize." He spoke again, John baptized in this river. Jesus' disciples baptized in this river. Why don't you baptize?" Again, this was all new to me, "Sir, I don't baptize."

Suddenly I was in the bible room at South Gate. The bible was open on the table and it seem to draw me to it. I read about baptizing in the river Jordan. I smelled a pleasant aroma and a breeze turned the pages. I looked at a map that showed the Sea of Galilee feeding the Jordan River that ran all the way to the Dead Sea. The aroma came again and the pages turned and I read Psalms 103:12 As far as the east is from the west, so far hath he removed our transgressions from us.

Suddenly I was back in the river. The man spoke again, "You must baptize. It is the water of separation. Satan will always try to remind them of their past." An older lady came alongside to be baptized, he took a handful of dirt from the river bottom and handed it to her, "This is your past. When I baptize you unto the Lord, let it go underwater." He baptized her and when she came up, she had a great big smile. He said, "every time you are reminded of your past, tell satan to go find it. It is washed as far as the east is unto the west. Into the Sea of Forgetfulness, The Dead Sea."

She walked away and he looked at me, "Where are your sins? Is your conscience clean?" Suddenly I was in a desert like place. There was sand all around. A tall sandy hill was in front of me and women in desert type robes were all around the base of the hill. They were talking among themselves and I moved closer to hear. They were talking about the man on top of the hill. They said he was the greatest archer that had ever lived. I looked up at the top of the hill and then back to them,

"Can I meet him?" They seemed frightened at my request and all of them began to back away from me. I turned again and looked at the top. I decided to climb. The hill was steep and sand squeezed between my finger as I dug into climb. I finally made it to the top. There was a man sitting on a peculiar type stick. It was in the shape of a 'T' and was belted to his bottom. He turned while sitting and I realized the stick was a hunting stool that allowed him to turn quietly. I asked softly, "Sir, will you teach me to shoot?" He stood up and handed me the bow. He took out an arrow out of his quiver, handed it to me and said, "SHOOT!" I was nervous but I readied the arrow and looked around for a target.

There was nothing but sand everywhere. All the ladies were gone and not even a footprint to aim at. I asked, "At what?" He became mad and snatched the bow out of my hand, "Come back when you are ready!"

Suddenly I was standing on the balcony, outside my room. I was sad and puzzled. I thought what the vision could mean. I looked at the circular calendar in the front drive. I saw Grandpa, "Grandpa, what does it mean?" He walked over to the angel with a bow, "If you aim at nothing, you'll get it. Faith is the substance of things hoped for. What are you aiming at?"

Suddenly I realized I had still had the arrow in my hand, "I am ready" I shouted. I was back on top of the hill, the Archer handed me the bow and said, "SHOOT!" I readied the arrow, this time I saw the map of the globe. He said, "I will give you dominion over the land you choose." I saw America and I did not hesitate. I let the arrow fly.

Chapter Eleven

Christmas Day

I woke to the sounds of people talking. I was in my room and the sun was just rising through the window. I sat up in bed and began thanking him for his grace and goodness. I had instant recall of the dream.

Suddenly I thought about the diaries. I jumped up and looked all around the bed. I looked under it, then the closets. I looked out on the balcony and then toward the calendar, but nothing. Finally, I got dresses and headed down the stairs. Sure, was a lot of noise coming from down stairs. I rounded the corner of the great room, "Grandma Fayth! Grandma Grace! Mom, Robert, everyone was there.

The place was packed, standing room only. Ryan came over and hugged me, "Merry Christmas. I hope you didn't sleep last night." We both laughed. Grandma Fayth began, "Lydia Fayth, I come to see you with those diaries. Have you received them yet?"

The room got deathly quiet, I thought about what Grandma and Grandpa had said. "No Ma'am. Grandma said they had never been outside the bloodline and she kept them hid under a stone. When I asked Grandpa, he said that the fragrance of Christ would guide me." Everyone stared at me and then back to Grandma Fayth. She said, Well, the bloodline is the

189

innocent blood of Jesus and we claimed this entire property protected by the blood, so they could be anywhere on the property.

Ryan asked, "Didn't the shadow man try to get in your room? Maybe they are in your room." "No Sir, combed every nook and cranny this morning.", I walked over and hugged mom and then grabbed Robert.

Grandma Grace broke in, "Then the blood line refers to the house because the demon of doubt couldn't cross it." Grandma Fayth joined in, "Okay, what stone?" We all started looking around. Kevin started shaking each stone in the fireplace wall. "Ryan, there are hundreds of stones in this house" Ryan nodded and started to help check for loose ones.

Robert questioned, "I'm a little out of place but what about the fragrance?" Everyone started looking at each other. Elizabeth yelled, "The Bible Room!" It was like a mad house as we all rushed the hallway. Grandma Fayth opened the door, "Child, you have to receive them." She walked in behind me followed by almost everyone.

The smell of almond filled the room and I scanned the room for a stone of some kind. My eyes fell on the engraved granite stones of the Ten Commandments. "The Ten Commandments", I said. We all stared. I looked at Ryan and Kevin, "Would you please?", I motioned toward the far wall where the stones were hung. Ryan looked to see how they were hung, "I can't see how they are up here." Kevin ran his fingers all the way around the edges, "It's like they were made in place." Grandma Grace said, "That granite came from Elberton, Georgia. That is solid and has to weigh over five hundred pounds." Ryan said, "I see something. Turn off the lights."

Robert was slightly behind me and found the switch. With the lights off, we could see a glow coming out from around the entire edge.

Grandma Fayth and I stepped closer. I looked at the engraved words, none of the commandments had a period except number five. Honor thy Father and Mother so thy days will be long upon the land. "There is a period after the fifth commandment." I reach out and pushed it. It was a button and the stone tablets jumped out just a little. "Grandma Fayth looked at Ryan, "Very careful and very slowly. Don't touch anything but the stones."

Ryan worked his fingers in behind the stones. He started pulling but it was too heavy. Kevin stepped up on the couch to help and so did Robert. They pulled and grunted and the stones slowly slide forward like a drawer. The stone tablets were a part of one large stone that had been carved into a complete drawer, attached to rollers and supported by cables.

Robert said, "Somebody was serious!" Ryan added, "Not only serious but very, very good." Kevin and Robert stepped down but Ryan leaned over and glanced inside. His face lit up and he was trying to say something as he just passed out.

Robert and Kevin tried to break his fall but all three ended up on the floor. Grandma Fayth asked, "Is he breathing?" Robert put his ear to Ryan's mouth. We all waited. "Yes Ma'am. He's breathing!" She continues, "Glory to God! He's just under."

About that time Grandma Grace lost it, screamed Glory and fell out. Grandpa John caught her and smiling, just sat her back on the couch and joined her. Grandma Fayth turned to me,

"Child, only you can touch them, you have to receive your gift then you can let us hold them." We both stepped forward and I stepped up on the couch. There was a glowing light coming out of the drawer and I couldn't see where it was coming from. I leaned over and looked in.

There it was, the leather bound, ancient style chest and light was coming from it. I began to shake uncontrollably. "What's wrong child?" Grandma asked. I looked at Grandma and back to the chest. Back to Grandma and then back to the chest. When I looked back to her again I said, "Grandma, I need to be Baptized, Now!"

Grandma turned toward the door, "Elizabeth, get the towels and blankets, we're going to the creek." Elizabeth and Katrina whirled and bolted up the steps. Grandma continued, "Robert, can you and Kevin close the vault?" "Yes Ma'am" they both said. She turned toward John, "Get her up. She needs to be with us." She took my hand and helped me to step down,

"Child, you are worth the wait!" She smiled as she reached down to recover Ryan. "Get up! Get up! She has to be baptized and I'm going to need your help." She looked up at me with one of those grins, "See why God chose women?" Ryan made it to a sitting position and Grandma Grace was doing pretty good as we walked into the great room.

The Baptism

We all made it to the creek, well below the greenhouse. I didn't feel any kind of guilt from a specific wrong doing, just an extreme sense of shame from seeing a self-centered me. I just seemed to know I was supposed to disconnect from the old life and begin my new life. My mind wouldn't quit picturing the bearded man in the Jordon River and all he had said to me. As Ryan, Grandma Fayth and I stepped down into the creek, I reached down and scooped up a handful of dirt. The winter water was bone chilling cold, I thought about Grandma Fayth's heart as she led me by the arm into the waist deep water. I had never felt water so cold but an urgency forced me to release and bury my past. Ryan's voice shivered as he began to speak, "Lord, we are here today to celebrate an enormous beginning. We come to deliver to you the birth of her spirit. The soul surrenders and as the water breaks, a spirit is born." He turned toward me and said, "I baptized you in the name of the Father, in the name of Jesus and in the name of the Holy Ghost." COLD! So cold! The water was so cold, it was like satan had clinched both his hands around my hand with the dirt. My hand did not want to open. Inside I was screaming but my hand wouldn't let go. It seemed forever but as I broke the water's surface, my hand opened and the old Lydia passed away. The sand passed away like time in a bottle. I heard cheers from the creek bank as we were met with towels and blankets.

The Diaries

Once in the house, it didn't take long before we were back in the bible room. Ryan and Kevin opened the stone vault and Grandma Fayth and I stepped up onto the couch. I reached in and lifted out the most beautiful leather-bound chest I had ever seen. The air was filled with the fragrance of almond, light came from the chest like diamonds under a lamp. Grandma and

Ryan helped me to sit down on the couch. Grandma looked up toward everyone and said, "We have to leave her alone for now."

And without any words, everyone left the room. I looked up to see Grandma Fayth and Mom smiling as the doors closed. I sat the chest on the couch next to me.

I couldn't believe what I had in my hands. I thought about how I was feeling. I felt a part of something way bigger than I could imagine but at the same time, I felt like I belonged. I wondered why I felt the need for baptism. It wasn't an unworthy or unclean feeling just a sense that I was supposed to. I sat for a long time just staring at the glow.

I rehearsed every word that Grandma and Grandpa had said about the diaries. Four generations, I thought, four generations of faith, work and expectations had all led to this. I imagined Grandma Fayth as a child running through the yard and Grandma Margaret looking out the window at her and then glancing back toward the carved stones. I imagined Grandma Grace running through the yard some years later and Grandma Fayth looking out the same window at her and then looking back at the stones. Then I saw Momma as a child, running the same way and Grandma Grace watching her and glancing back to the stones.

I thought about each of my Grandfathers and then about Dad. I thought about how Dad named me, how my name meant Trust and that now God was placing trust in me by giving me the secrets of the women. I couldn't wait any longer so I reached to open the chest. Somehow, I knew everything was about to change but unlike the tornado I had been in, this time I know the driver.

194

I lifted the lid and the light was so bright that I was light blinded for a moment. My eyes adjusted and I counted nine diaries and a bunch of what looked like sheets of cloth type paper. There were two dried plants, stems of some kind, laying on top of the folded leather-bound diaries and a very old cup with writing on it that I could not understand.

Each of the plants had a small cloth type note attached, rolled up on their stem and tied with what looked like a blade of grass. I picked up the first one and carefully untied the blade. The paper was very dry and cloth like and the writing on it said, "Ra'ah maqqel shaqed", "I see, a rod, of an almond tree". The note continued, 'The almond tree is of great importance to our Father. The word "almond" comes from a word "shakad" which means "watch" or "wake".

It is the first tree to bloom in the spring and proclaims a great awakening from a winter sleep. It was Aaron's rod that bloomed and bore fruit in the middle of an Israelite winter. The blooms are so breath taking that our Father decorated the Menorah with the oil cups in the shape of it. God asked Jeremiah, "what do you see?". Jeremiah answered, "I see an almond branch", then God said, "You have seen well, I am watching over my word to perform it." There were three things in the ark of the covenant, the stone tablets, Aaron's rod and the manna which was the bread of life. The rod of an almond is given to the watchman, and this one is delivered to you, the time of awakening is here.'

One minute I would tremble and the next I would feel extreme heat come over me. As I looked at the rod, I noticed tiny green shoots. I thought my eyes were playing tricks on me, I looked very closely and there was definitely, new growth!

I carefully placed it back in the chest and picked up the next stem. I untied the blade and began to read, 'Qaneh, a Reed. The stem you are holding is what made the papyrus you are reading. It is made with the inner stem of this reed. We lay strips, side by side and then lay a second layer crossing them. After they dry we hammer them tight and soften them with a stone. This is what we write our words on.

This was a gift from Mary, the wife of Peter. She gave it to me and explained, the name Simon meant reed and the first day Simon met our Lord, Jesus said, "No longer will you be called Simon, a reed but your name will be Cephas, a stone." She said that Jesus took the inner bark of the reed, the spirit, and hardened it into a stone to place his word upon the hearts of man.

To her, Peter was the papyrus, the converted reed. May the Lord use you to write his word in your day.' I stared at the small stem and smiled as I thought how Grandma Margaret must have loved this plant.

I laid it down and looked at the diaries. I sensed the order of the binders were from left to right so I pulled out the first one. Carved into the front leather was, "Lydia, Porphyropolis", the seller of purple. I rubbed my hand across the binding. I could feel an energy and it made my insides shake, like every nerve in my body was expecting something big.

I opened up the binder and the papyrus scrolls had been flattened into what we would call a legal-size paper.

Lydia's Diary

The papyrus was dated, 1st day of the Planting Moon, 44th Year of our Lord. It began, "Lord, I pray for sister Salome. I received word today that her son, our beloved Disciple James was beheaded by order of Herod Agrippa. I also pray for blessings upon his accuser's family. It was said that the accuser was so moved by James' spirit that he fell to the ground at James' feet and received you and that both James and the accuser came home to be with you, with smiles on their faces. I pray that James' younger brother John is well and that his work is going as you desire. As you know Lord, Timon and Parmenas both were martyred today, one at Philipi and the other at Macedonia. As I meditate upon my coming to you, I am torn between to loves. All that is in me desires to be with you but at the same time my heart longs to continue to teach your children the Way and how to pray. All our sisters feel the same way so I have begun collecting their words, that somehow, you may use them to reach children we will never see, this side of Heaven. Each of the sisters have a specific teaching because you taught them yourself, after you came back from the tomb. Even though I wasn't in the Upper Room, I know the calling you have given me and what I say to people today and what I would say to children of future generations; 'My name is Lydia. It means trust and that is what I offer you today. If you will allow me into your heart, I will never leave you nor forsake you. Trust is the only foundation that a relationship, a love and covenant can be built upon. I am a business woman and trust is easy to give but sometimes hard to find because the will of man can change. Who you trust today, may not be who you can trust tomorrow and a faithful person maybe hard to find. The best way to know if you can trust a man is to know his will and I have spent my life examining the Will of God, and have built my relationship with him, upon this trust. If you want to know the will of God, let him speak for himself. If God said, "I Will." then I do not believe you could stop him, I do not think the king can stop him nor do I think the devil can stop him and here is what he said he will do.

I will not again curse the ground.

I will establish my covenant with you.

I will look upon the rainbow and remember our covenant.

I will bless you.

I will bless all the work of your hand.

I will bless your house.

I will bless your businesses.

I will bless your food.

I will bless your body.

I will bless your children.

I will bless them that bless you and curse them that curse you.

I will make you exceedingly fruitful.

I will be with you and not leave you.

I will go before you.

I will do you good.

I will bring you out of affliction.

I will bring you out from under burdens.

I will be with your mouth to teach you what to say.

I will rid you of bondage.

I will redeem you and take you for my own.

I will be your God.

I will smite your enemies.

I will send my fear to your enemies.

I will make all your enemies turn and run.

I will send an Angel before you.

I will take sickness away from you.

I will give you rest.

I will heal you.

I will command my blessing upon you.

I will give you rain in due season.

I will bless your fields.

I will bless your crops.

I will bless your harvest.

I will teach thee, instruct thee and guide thee.

I will not fail thee.

I will hasten after my word to perform it.

Call unto me and I will answer thee and show thee wonderful and mighty things.

I will make you fishers of men.

Trust in the Lord, it is a rock that holds firm in your spirit and will energize your soul. Never let it be said again, "If it is God's will", for you are without excuse, you have heard his will. Read these thirty-eight declarations, made with his own lips, every day and every night just before you pray and you will always know the Will of God. Trust is what your Faith is built upon, do not neglect laying a strong foundation under your tower of prayers.' Lord, this is my offering to you for generations to come. Teach them the Way to your love and teach them to Pray. Amen" I closed the leather binding as her words jumped into my heart. I thought how totally impossible it would be for someone or something to stop God from doing what he said he would. I realized the strength that my grandparents had from knowing this but I also knew there must be a power hidden in the combination of diaries because this one, alone, wasn't going to stop the dark times ahead. I leaned forward and pulled out the next diary. There was a small paper attached to the front, a note from Grandma Margaret, "I have attached a brief introduction for each diary to help you know who it is and what type person it was who wrote them. Joanna was a strong woman of position and wealth. She was married to Chuza, Herod's servant and she supported Jesus with her substance." I held up the diary, this one felt different. The leather binding was the same type but the energy coming from this one was way off the scale. It was like holding electric light beams in my hands that sent a charge through my body from the tingling in my hair to a burning on the soles of my feet. The energy was so great that I stood up and began to pace back and forth. I tried several times to open the binder but the energy wouldn't let me.

My Prayer

Finally, I sat down and began to pray. I closed my eyes and it wasn't long before I was in the inner court of prayer. I could heart my heart racing and my quick, short breaths. It was dark and I asked, "Lord, why can't I receive the diary? Is there a key?" Suddenly there was a box floating down and landed in front of me. It was the present that had been between the bull and the baby and had a large deep red ribbon wrapped around the box and tied into a bow. I reached down and pulled at the end on the ribbon. It gently came untied and slipped off the box. As the box opened, a great explosion of light came out and it forced me to open my eyes, I was looking at Joanna's diary. The energy I had been feeling was still there but somehow it had surrendered to the light from the box. I opened the diary and began to read.

Joanna's Diary

"There is a scarlet red ribbon that binds the old covenant and our new covenant into one whole and wraps together the hearts of all believers, past, present and future. A ribbon so simple that even a child can untie it and understand, and yet it's strength so profound that kings cannot break it nor comprehend it. It can neither be bought or sold, nor borrowed or lent. It is a gift from the owner and must be received by the heart. God offered Abraham a covenant and Abraham did enter in. It is not the covenant of Abraham nor was it Abraham blessing God. It is God's covenant, he is the author and the finisher, the Alpha and the Omega. As you well know, when you enter an agreement with someone, you examine the benefits. When you see that the benefits are great, you quickly try to close the deal by paying. If the benefits are so great as to bless your family and your generations to come, you know your payment must reflect your full, life-long commitment. God offered Abraham blessings that were so great that it was beyond Abraham's ability to pay. When Abraham considered what his greatest treasure was, he set out to give God his son. As we well know, God was pleased by Abraham's intent but held his hand from harming the son and provided a substitute. The scarlet ribbon had forever bound the hearts of God and Abraham. It is well known when two parties enter a covenant that every transaction must be balanced and equal, and that every sincere intent must be met with the same. We do not know whether it was wisdom on the part of Abraham to offer his son or if it was the wisdom of God that required him to do so. What we do know was God bound himself to send a Messiah. Abraham offered his son, God bound himself to offer his. All our prophets and scribes have written of his coming. Our scriptures confound the wise and confuse the learned. They study and study, they memorize and theorize of the complexity and analyze their intent. They try to apply small fragments to their lives as one who adorns jewelry. All the while God ordains praise from the mouth of babes, even a child can understand a covenant partner, can understand truth, honesty and love. Our hearts, the little child inside each of us, knew he was coming but wondered what he would look like. It was said that a virgin would bring forth the child, but how could we be sure? Did you know her? It was said he would remove burdens and destroy yokes but haven't you been helped by others? It was said the lame would walk and the blind would see but did we know them? Were they really lame or really blind? It was said that death could not hold him and that he would rise from the grave in three days? Now this would be a sure test if it was the Messiah, the son of God sent by the covenant agreement. By this one act alone, the scarlet red ribbon of the covenant blood could not be denied. I was there when it was said a virgin has had a child. I have met the virgin. I was there when burdens were removed and yokes destroyed. I have seen the lame leap and dance for joy. I have watched in amazement as the blind describe their new world in glorious detail. I have shared the tears of joy with countless thousands of the healed but could it be him? I was there the day he was beaten beyond recognition, with no part that was not covered in blood. I was there when he was nailed to the cross and I was there when he was taken down. And I was there with the others as we held our breath for three days. Was it him? Could it be?

Abraham, oh father Abraham, we only have use of your blessings by the covenant you made. He has said we can enter the covenant anew, with him. Can it be the covenant Son, the Messiah foretold? I say unto you, I WAS THERE! I was there when he walked into the room! I was there when we touched the holes in his feet and hands. I was there when we touched his spear pierced side and I was there when we held his crown of thorns. I have set at the feet of the undeniable Son of God, the Messiah, the promised fulfillment of God's covenant with Abraham. And I am here to show you the Way to enter in to God's covenant love with his Son. His name is Jesus and we are his body of believers. We are bound by the honor of the scarlet red ribbon of the blood of the only begotten son of God, to bring to you his offered covenant. Just as God offered a covenant to Abraham, Jesus is offering you a covenant by his own blood. He taught us that the covenant body is a family, that taking care of one another, helping and giving to one another was love. He taught us that God was our Father, that he is love and that we have to be born of the spirit of love to enter into his family. All that are born of this spirit, must die to self. To some this is easy but to others it is a very hard thing but as I said earlier, one must examine the benefits. Jesus said "Ask, and you will receive. Seek, and you shall find. Knock, and the door shall be opened unto you." He said, "Ask anything in my name and you shall have it, so when you pray, believe that you receive and you shall have it." and, "All things are possible to them that believe." All the promises of God and the promises of the Son are yours and Jesus promised us to live forever with him in the palaces of Heaven. Two things must be dealt with at this point. First, if you live beneath the promises, you have no one to blame but yourself for the failure to pray. Prayer is exercising your faith in the promises. Second, there are many churches being formed that claim Jesus as their Lord so, I find it necessary to give you an example that will allow you to know a body of believers who have entered covenant with Jesus, compared to those that have entered a covenant with a church or another man. The easiest and most telling example is their use of the covenant giving or tithe. God said to bring the tithe into the storehouse and see if he would not pour out a blessing that you do not have room enough to hold. The primary purpose of our tithes is for the welfare of our people. We are a city to ourselves. A joint food storage that replaces the need to use the Roman markets. Our Disciple Matthew was a toll collector and he describes it as a user fee. You must pay a toll to enter the city and often another toll to enter the markets. This is why, many of our brothers and sister are martyred. The law expresses that Rome is the Deity which means that all your blessing come from the government and you cannot serve another King. When we establish a body of believers in a town, they soon become targeted for interfering with the roman markets. But as believers we will not deny Jesus as Lord and King, and I and all our covenant will gladly give our bodied for our family and our covenant storehouse because it is right, it is just and it is love. Jesus taught us that we are developing the Kingdom of God, here on earth. First in our family, then our community and then our territory and by caring for others, we would always have more than enough. I have found this to be so. Our body of believers use the tithe for our food store, like an investment partnership, where all of our covenant members receive food at liberty, at no cost and without shame, because their tithe has supplied it. The store is cared for by our elderly that are beyond their working years but many of our members enjoy helping.

We also have a long term food storage plan, modeled after God's wisdom demonstrated in the story of Joseph. Second thing our tithe is used for is elderly planning. Income units are acquired so that when we are beyond our working years, there will be more than enough for our constant growing body of believers. An income unit may be livestock, or fruit trees or even lease properties, but it is all jointly owned by the entire tithing body and its sole purpose is to provide for the body. Now, in contrast, I have heard that many churches use the tithes to support a preacher and even using the tithe to feed his donkeys. One church that I know of even uses the tithe to supply the pastor with a chariot and horses so that his church may be recognized as blessed by God. All the while, some of his tithing members, who had tithed faithfully for years, have fallen on hard times and when they asked the deacons for help, they were shamed for not believing in God, and turned away. My friends, this is not the covenant that Jesus taught us, this is a covenant with an idea. The tithe has to flow in both directions or you are not building a covenant body, you are building a man. God's stated purpose in the covenant with Abraham was to reach the children. Jesus coming to fulfill the covenant did not remove God's purpose, he amplified it. Our duty is to teach the children the way to the covenant of love and teach them to pray. Jesus said that all that come to him have been drawn by the Father and he will receive you. He said we must be born of the spirit of love, pass through the waters of separation and take of the cup of fellowship. If you are being drawn by the scarlet red ribbon of God, the blood-stained belt of his Son, then hesitate not, step forward." My heart was pounding so hard I didn't know if I should stand, run or just die. Electricity ran through me like lightening in a thunderstorm, like a metal pinball in a power plant. I didn't feel like I was in a tornado, I was the tornado! I wanted to scream, I got it! I understand the Bible! That's the reason People can't get it, the veil over their eyes! The whole book is about a love covenant! Building a viable, economically strong, body of believers! She's right! She's right! Amen! Amen! Amen! My hands and arms where shaking so that I almost couldn't close the diary. I slid it back into its place and grabbed the next one. I thought, I don't know how much more I can take, but light me up! I could feel the energy coming from the third diary but I didn't slow down. I looked at the leather cover, "Mary Magdalene". My heart seemed to skip four or five beats. A serious tone settled over the whole room. I felt I wasn't alone. I stopped and looked around, even though I knew there wasn't anyone there. This was real strange, I could sense her there. I looked at the couch across from me, expecting to see her. I stared for a moment and at one point, I started to ask her a question out loud. I caught a whiff of what smelled like sweat mixed with something I couldn't recognize. Finally, I looked at her diary, opening it I felt like crying? Wow! What a rollercoaster. I closed it and looked back at the couch. When I felt I was ready, I opened it and began. This one was different, it had several short entries.

Mary Magdalene Diary

"Oh God, help me. I am confused. Your priest said I was good, he said I was clean because he had offered sacrifice for me and he took me to his bedchamber. He used me and then he threw me out into the street. I had no clothes, they all had stones and I was about to die. They called a man to judge me and his words laid upon their hearts until they all dropped their stones and none would cast the first. He asked me where were my accusers and when I looked, there were none. He said neither did he condemn me and he gave me a robe. He said, 'Sister, go in peace.' I ran from him as fast as I ever ran. He has frightened me greater than any fear I have ever known. I am confused oh Lord. Why did he call me sister? Who is the man? He is not my brother. What does he want from me?" The smell of fright and sweat was strong. I could feel it rising off the papyrus scroll and as I looked closer, I could see where drops had landed on the scroll and had dried. I turned to the next entry and continued. This time there was a complete different smell that I didn't recognize at all. It was very odd, the scents from the last entry didn't seem to overlap this scent. "Oh Lord, I have never wore, such a robe so fine. Everyone has noticed it and they are treating me different. Everyone is talking about a prophet who has come to town. He is dining with the Pharisees tonight. I hope to meet him alone to share my kindness. I will carry this alabaster box of ointment to anoint his chamber." I placed my nose closer to the papyrus to get a better smell. I still couldn't recognize the aroma but it made me think of spring time and it had a tantalizing spicy drift that seemed to linger. I turned to the next entry. "Oh God, I am sorry. I have never felt the weight of shame. I have never known the axe of righteousness and I have never seen love divide a world as lightening divides a night sky. Have I fallen so far that your arms can not reach me? Hear my cries oh Lord, I am broken. I am blind and I am not able to stand in the presence of your prophet. They said his name was Jesus. I entered the house of the Pharisee and came up behind him. I thought to myself that I would anoint his head so his thoughts would carry me until we could meet alone. When he turned, I saw him. It was the man who called me 'Sister'. My mind pictured the week before, naked in the street about to die. My legs would not hold the weight of my sins for he held my heart of love in one hand and he knew my sins and held them in the other. He covered my nakedness and cloaked my sin with his covering just as you did for Adam and Eve, in the garden. My shame came over me like a mighty wave and I had no place to hide. I fell to his feet and all I could do was weep, and weep, and weep. I was suddenly aware that my tears were covering his feet and I tried frantically to dry them with my hair. All I had to say thank you with was the ointment in the alabaster box. I kissed his feet and anointed them. Oh God, bless this man all the days of his life! I must meet him again and ask him why." I knew I had read this story in the Bible before but I never realized the pattern applied to the garden story. I remembered Grandpa John saying that the old covenant reflected the new and Joanna's diary said they were bound together. I thought for a moment, so much for calculus and quantum algebra, the Bible is way more than a man written story book of history. Each of her entries just drove me to the next. As I turned to the next papyrus, I had become accustom to finding a new aroma. This one had the fragrance of almond and, the diary and the bible room just seemed to blend as I opened the next entry. "Oh Lord, Jesus was at the river Jordan today and his disciples were baptizing the people. I trembled as I approached him but I had to ask him why. Why he helped me, why he gave me the robe and why he called me 'Sister'? When I was allowed to see him, I could barely speak, I could not look him in the eyes. I just hung my head down and as I handed him back his robe, I somehow got the words out, 'Why did you call me sister?' His voice was like thunder and a gentle breeze, both at the same time. He said, 'The robe is yours and you are my sister.' I looked up at him and said I don't understand. He stared at me and questioned, 'Don't you want to be the sister of the Son of God?' I thought I was going to faint. He said, 'Sister, sins are things you have done in the past. If you could start over today, washing away the past and being born again clean, would you?' I said yes but how? He pointed toward the river, 'The waters of separation. Put off the old man and put on the new. Bury Mary Magdalene the sister of sins and be born Mary Magdalene the Sister of Jesus, the Son of Righteousness. Will you be my sister?' I nodded and walked with him down to the river. His disciple John reached and took my hand. Oh Lord, today I have died and yet I live. Bless my brother all the days of his life." I thought about being baptized earlier this morning and about what the Lord had taught me in the vision. I wondered why I felt the need to be baptized before I touched the diaries. I turned to the next papyrus, it was her final entry. I could smell flowers and I had a sense of a multitude of children singing and dancing. I began to read, "Lord, I have learned so much over the past couple of years. The sisters and I have set ourselves to write what each of us believe to be important and would leave for the generations to come. I have chosen baptism and I believe there are several important things they should know. In the story of Noah, you separated the old world of sin, from the new world, by water. Then in the temple you created the water of separation to divide that which is clean from that which is unclean. Even the priest must pass through the water of separation before he can serve you in the temple. It is the laver in the temple that holds the water and it is called the pulpit. You taught us that we are cleaned by the washing of the word and that when a child is born, it is the breaking of the water that allows it to pass from one life into another. That is why you fulfilled all righteousness when you had John the Baptist, baptize you before you entered in to ministry for the father. And that is why we must pass through the water to separate from our old life and begin a new life in the covenant of love." There it was, the reason I felt the need to be baptized before touching the diaries. I thought for a moment how her life changed when she entered a covenant as described by Joanna. My mind thought about the dark times ahead and how a true covenant would far surpass anything a government would be capable of doing, especially in a collapse of the monetary systems. I thought for a moment how Jesus was way smarter than what I had been led to believe by the hippy dippy crowd. When he was talking to the man with the barns about entering in to the covenant, he wasn't saying, "Join us, this is the love and kindness generation." He was talking to one of the largest bankers in town. All barn owners were bankers. Barns were where farmers stored their grain and the barn owner received a percentage of the storage. Jesus was having a, serious values meeting with the top banker of that day and let him have it, right between the eyes. Jesus was building an empire, a real factual economic kingdom built by entering a covenant of love. No wonder governments like China reject Christianity. America has too, that is the kind that Joanna spoke about.

Susanna's Diary

I closed her leather and reached for the next. I just couldn't stop. The note attached from Grandma read, " Susanna was also a woman of business and substance. She and Joanna supported and cared for Jesus' needs. It is likely they were sisters but we are not sure." I looked at the leather that held her diary. Etched into the front surface was a large cup and on it was the name Susanna. I could detect a smell of moisture, like an early spring dew. That smell you seem to get every spring when, one day, you walk out of your house and you realize, spring has arrived. The leather-bound papyruses had a gentle glow coming from their edges and the energy I felt made me feel like something was beginning. It made me think of the almond branch and I glanced over at it. When I opened it, I was surprised. The artful penmanship was startling. I had never seen anything like this in all my years of school or in Washington, and I had seen all our founding documents on parchment. It drew my attention, to its importance, even greater as I stood up to walk and began to read. "Lord, As I set my hand to write to generations to come, I get a sense, in my spirit, that you would have me address one person, in the future, maybe a teacher or even a mother, that will seed a generation. I pray that I will fill her cup of fellowship as Elijah filled the widow's cruse. Amen. To my Daughter in Christ, God did not let any of Samuel's words fall to the ground, neither shall yours. Have you taken of the cup of the covenant? If not, I am sure you will be soon. I am giving you my most treasured possession, the cup of our Lord from the last supper. I have always kept it with me after having the room cleaned that evening." I began to tremble, I scrambled back to the chest. I saw the cup through swelling tears. I couldn't believe what I was seeing! Could this really be the cup? It had to be but. . . My hands were trembling as I touched the cup. Every fiber, from head to toe, was trembling as I held it to my chest. Just the thought of Jesus and each Disciple taking the cup of the new covenant had my mind spinning. I don't know how long I sat there but at some point, I realized I had been in a long daze. I carefully sat the cup back into the chest and picked up Susanna's diary and began again. "To enter in to covenant with our Lord, you must take of the cup of the covenant. It is necessary to enter in to fellowship with the believers. In times of old, when a covenant was made, two people would cut their hands and then shake, becoming blood brothers. What belonged to one brother, also belonged to the other and likewise for the other brother. After that, it became the custom to cut the hand and each person would drop three drops of blood into a glass of wine and both people would drink from the glass. Jesus said, "This cup is my blood of the new covenant which is shed for the remission of sin." When you take of the covenant cup, you have entered the family. Jesus is your blood brother, if you need him, he is there. and if he needs you, you are there. The same goes with those you enter in to covenant with, when you need, they are there and when they need, you are there. If not, then you do not have a covenant. What you have is an arrangement. Jesus said, "there is never a greater need than when someone has fallen and the well do not need a physician." Let me illuminate the cup in a parable of mine. There was a woman who was giving birth to a child. First signs that the time is near is contractions and labor pains. Soon, these become more frequent until that all seem to join into one furious tornado of confusion and turmoil. Finally, the water breaks and a child is born. Often, with the assistance of a midwife, the cord is cut, the breath of life comes and the child is handed to the mother for warmth and nourishment. Now let us examine the parallel, first a person finds themselves in labor and need or their order of daily life has begun contracting. Soon this labor and contractions become a tornado of feelings and emotions, possibly compounded by poor choices and bad relationships. Finally, their soul comes to the water of separation to somehow wash away the memories of who they once were. To cleanse the "I AM" in their spirit from the wardrobe choices of their soul. The water breaks as they are baptized and a spirit child is born. A clean and pure "I AM" spirit. Sometimes with assistance, the Lord cuts the cord. The thing that connects you to those people or things or habits. They may be your family, God told Abram to leave his father's house, or they could be people of relationships. But the cord must be cut! Many fall-away because they have one foot in their old world and one foot in the new, so whatever you do, cut the cord. Lastly, you are given the cup of the covenant. The cup of fellowship, of family and of his nourishment, his word. If the new born spirit is not fed, it will die. What you put in the cup, will be what you get out of the cup. We are changed into his image by staring at his face. Changed into his character by studying his words. Just as you are studying what the sisters have written, you are filling the cup. The more you fill, the more you grow. The more you fill, the stronger you become. May your cup always be filled with light and may your hunger and thirst never be filled. A child that is full will leave the table. I pray that this parable will serve you well as you become a faith coach and that you will lead a multitude into the covenant of the Lord. Our Lord told us, "If you love me, then keep my commandments." So I am giving you a few so your cup will not be empty. He said, "Love thy neighbor as thy self. Forgive and you shall be forgiven. Give and it shall be given. Do not pray for attention. Do not call your brother a fool. Repent and enter the New Covenant. Go, make disciples and baptize." Fill your cup, my child, fill your cup so you may nourish others in that day. God's peace be yours for today I will be with him. This will be the last time I quill this side of my heavenly home for Herod Agrippa has ordered our judgment." Her signature was so elegant I thought it must have been written by an angel. One part of me wanted to cry as if I had lost a sister while the other part longed to hug her. Her parable made me understand the Lord's table in a complete new light and at the same time, I sure could relate to the tornado and journey. I placed her diary back in order and gently rubbed the cup of the Lord, knowing she took of the same and that I would be also, in short order.

Mary's Diary, sister of Lazarus,

I drew out the next diary and read the attached note from
Grandma, "This Mary is the sister of Lazarus who was raised
from the dead. She also was the one who complained to Jesus
about Martha, her sister, sitting at the feet of Jesus while she
worked in the house." I looked at the leather and a tiny set of
praying hands was on the front and written beneath it was,
"Forsake Not the Little Children to Come unto Me". I'm not
sure why but this one felt light as a feather. It was the same
size, with a few papyruses but it was noticeably lighter. As I
opened the leather, a highly visible, light blue glow came of the
scroll. Like a light shining through a thin blue lamp shade but
not having a single source like a lamp, the light came evenly
from off the scroll. I began reading, "Lord, someone has to do
the work. I know you said that listening to you was better than
being busy working, but that was before you left us and told us
to go make disciples of all people. Now we have a church full
of listeners but very few doers. Help us reach the children Lord.
You commanded us not to forsake the children. God, our
Father, cut covenant with Abraham because he would teach his
children the way. Lord, the harvest is plenty but laborers are
few and I see it as my job to teach them to pray. The sisters
have decided to make record each of our hearts and at the
request of Lydia of Macedonia, gathered together to be passed
on to those that love more than themselves. After careful

meditation, if I were to leave anything to my grandchildren in faith, it would be the most powerful thing a believer has, the power of prayer. Lord, I pray that in the days to come that you will wrap words around that which is in my heart and my quill may capture the power you gave us, in such a way, that they may receive power from on high. Amen." My mind hung on every word and the energy I felt was like a train that was just getting started. I could sense motion in the right direction but deep inside I knew this, slow moving train was picking up speed and I had the feeling that it was going to be moving really, really fast. I turned to the next entry and began reading, "Lord, my heart longs to explain the infinite riches and value of prayer but words cannot capture the expressions there of. How do I explain to my daughters it is the source of your power that you have given them? How do I explain to them it is the thread that connects you to them, the bond between the two of you. How do I explain that if they do not speak to you daily, there is not a connection? Do they not speak to their mates or children daily? How can I explain that the word, 'glory' means to shine outward and that by answering prayers you are showing your power, your strength and your glory to the world through them? How can I tell them, "little prayer means little glory"? How can I tell them that prayers are arrows that pierce the darkness? How will they come to know that when you gave them the power of prayer that it means you gave them authority? That you left them in charge of your glory. Are they bound by ignorance or blinded by tradition in that they pray like beggars? Can they only see the value when the child is sick, when they are without money or when a disaster comes? At that very moment they only catch the tiniest glimpse of its value and yet they would gladly trade all they had for just one answered prayer in their moments of need. How can I reach their hearts with this light? How can I start an ember within their hearts from the raging fire within mine? How can I mother, oh Lord? How can I birth? You said, life and death are in the power of the tongue. By words man fell and by words he will be redeemed. You said, by our words we would be justified. You said, the sower went out to sow seeds and you said that words were seeds. So, by your words I will seed the ember and by your Spirit you will fan the flames. A King cannot lie and a blood bound oath or promise can never be broken. He said, What things so ever you desire, when you pray, believe you receive them, and you shall have them. He said, Ask and you shall receive. He said, Seek, and you shall find. He said, Knock, and the door shall be opened unto you. He said, all that ask, receive. All that seek, find. And all that knock, the doors shall be opened. He said, and all things, whatsoever ye shall ask in prayer, believing, ye shall receive. He said, and whatsoever ye shall ask in my name, that will I do, that the Father may be glorified in the Son. He said, if ye abide in me, and my words abide in you, ye shall ask what ye will, and it shall be done unto you. Herein is my Father glorified, that ye bear much fruit; so, shall ye be my disciples. He said, and in that day ye shall ask me nothing. Verily, verily, I say unto you, Whatsoever ye shall ask the Father in my name, he will give it you. He said, call unto me and I will answer you. He said, for verily I say unto you, that whosoever shall say unto this mountain, Be thou removed, and be thou cast into the sea; and shall not doubt in his heart, but shall believe that those things which he saith shall come to pass; he shall have whatsoever he saith. Therefore, I say unto you, What things so ever ye desire, when ye pray, believe that ye receive them, and ye shall have them. He said, if you can believe, all things are possible to him that believeth. He said, Verily, verily, I say unto you, He that believeth on me, the works that I do shall he do also; and greater works than these shall he do; because I go unto my Father. And whatsoever ye shall ask in my name, that will I do, that the Father may be glorified in the Son. If ye shall ask any thing in my name, I will do it. Lord, that is my seed to the daughters of the future. You said, we have not, because we ask not. I am asking, in your name, by the blood bound covenant promises, that all that read this become baptized in your love and become ministers of this word, forever. Amen." Tears were burning my cheeks and my head was so hot it felt as if a furnace had been lit in the room. I laid the leather back in place as my eyes were blinking, trying to regain focus. Every word found a place in my heart. His words, his promises and his declarations were forever carved in my memory and I was beginning to feel like the train. I sat for a while processing everything I had gleaned so far. Lydia laid a foundation of Trust with what God said, "I will do." Joanna illuminated what a Covenant was and wasn't. Mary Magdalene carried my understanding to the Waters of Separation and entering the covenant. While Susanna opened my eyes to the Birth of a Spirit and the Lord's Cup. Now I have filled my cup with the Power, Glory and Strength of God by Mary, the sister of Lazarus. I felt an energy that I had never felt before, like a jet about to take off. There is a power from deep within that seems to be saying, "What next? Point me at something! Shoot! Shoot!" I thought about the vision of the Archer where he handed me the bow and said, "Shoot!" I knew I was his and he was mine. I knew we were joined and he had handed me his bow, his power, his glory. And anything I wanted to shoot at I was going to hit and win. Not only do I feel this power but I also feel a nervous energy. Something like a runner waiting on the starting gun. I reached for the next diary and as I touched the leather, I instantly knew everything was about to change. I had a strong taste of caffeine in the back of my throat which was odd because I drank coffee very seldom. It was similar to an energy drink kind of feeling I would get around the office when everything was jumping.

Martha's Dairy

I adjusted myself on the couch, looked at the leather-bound diary and smiled. The etching was that of an Archer with his bow drawn and written under it was one word, Faith. Grandma's note just said, "Martha is the other sister of Lazarus." I opened it and began, "Lord, the class is going well and the children are learning your Disciple Ship Illustration and Parable perfectly. You make it so easy to apply our faith to all areas of life that most of the adults are using the Disciple Ship as the basic outline for their Faith Plans. I do have a few questions about teaching priorities for different age groups and I also have a few questions from some of the students. I'm going to run through your teaching outline and ask our questions as I get to each one, that way I can keep everything in its proper order and my questions will be in my diary so I can review as you illuminate them to me. First, you taught us that God was our Father and that each of us have four areas he gives us authority in. When you were teaching us on the mountainside, you instructed us on how to use our faith concerning our self, concerning our family, concerning our society and concerning God, our Father. You taught us to have a Faith Plan and that all things were possible through Faith. Then, when you taught us by the sea, you instructed us that these four areas were like sailing a ship with four masts, one for each area of our lives and that the sails were our prayers in each of the areas. You called it a Disciple Ship and said that it would be very difficult to sail a ship without any sails. You said that nothing could stop one prayer but an organized group of prayers was like a ship in full sail. You said that the first mast was named "Self" and that each of us had to have sails on that masts, from what we wanted to learn, to whatever we desired, places we wanted to go or even people we wanted to meet. But the prayers, like sails, carried us in a direction. You also taught us that children have to start their faith voyage with this one mast and as they grow, their ship would grow each of the other masts at the proper time. That is our first question, when is the proper time to add the second mast of family? Many of our children are beginning to pray for their families at an early age. A what point do we help them to gather the strength of both masts and the abundance of sails? Some pray for a family member's birthday and others for health or blessings but it appears by age seven that they should add the second mast. The third mast seems to come naturally when a person begins equity matters. The mast of Society, how to do business or treat neighbors and enemies. This mast is usually the largest with a grand array of sails. Prayers are exercising Faith and when doing business our adults, both young and old have great faith. You taught us that Faith was a method of exchange that no money or coin could replace or compare. That by faith we were made whole, by faith we prosper, are enlarged and saved. That faith was the substance of things hoped for, the goals and destinies of life. You said that no one arrives at a destination by accident and that every ship owner must be headed toward something and have a plan of navigation. You also taught us how to tell when a storm is coming and how to adjust our sails. This is where most of us have questions. Every indicator you taught us points to a serious storm and we know that we must pull in many of our sails and hold fast to the sails on the fourth mast. The mast call Kingdom, where our prayers for the Church and the Kingdom on earth are placed. There is so much we need to learn and to pass on before we enter this storm. Salome has told us of the days ahead and also, of many years to come, but it is our desire that we leave the knowledge of how to develop a Faith Plan and build a Disciple Ship, to the children of the future. We can have them draw out a ship with four tall masts. We can have them list their prayers on each one. Prayers for Self, for Family, for Business and for God, but what we can't do is balance their ship. To much Self and they will crash on the rocks. To much Family and they will fail to manifest your glory. To much Business and they will lose the precious cargo of family. That will take the wisdom of those teachers that walk by faith. Those that have speaking faith, that call those things that be not as though they were, those that speak to a mountain and the mountain moves. Lord, we can teach them but you will have to send people to coach them. To build them up in your most Holy Faith. Lord, send Faith Coaches to teach the children for the Kingdom's sake. This is the last prayer on top of our mast called Kingdom. Our other masts will be broken by the storm ahead but as our ships cross the sea to enter your Kingdom, let our last prayer be tethered to the mast by your love for them. Amen." I slowly closed the leather, my mind operating like a mathematical catalog, adding up exchange rate values. A prayer for healing, what would it be worth? A prayer for a car or a house? How about a prayer for a new born child from a woman who couldn't have one, what would the value be? I remembered the story of Grandma Margaret and her prayer atop Cohutta Mountain, the reason I am here and the reason for these diaries. What's the value? I could see what Jesus meant when he said it was a method of exchange that money couldn't compare or replace. I thought for a moment, if I were going through the fall of the American economy, wars and sickness for the next fourteen years, this is a Kingdom economy that would work. I could clearly see that learning to pray was just a starting point and that organizing your prayers in distinct areas truly empowered. I smiled as I thought how women were better multitask organizers and I seemingly realized why God had chosen women to carry Faith Coaching to the future. I finally realized that faith was not complicated, just complex and yet, very simple. For the first time since I receive Grandma's letter, I felt I had a handle on this and I finally had something to offer others and do for myself. As I placed the diary back in the chest and drew out the next, my mind was already sorting out my own faith plan in vivid detail.

Mary, wife of Peter

Grandma's note said, "Strong men most often have very strong wives. Peter's wife Mary is no exception." I looked at the etching on the leather. It was a square ended sword of some kind and written below was the words, "The Sword of Peter". As I opened the papyrus I recalled the reed and Mary's note on how the papyrus was made. She began, "Lord, you told us many times that a prayer must pass through the outer court to get into the inner court and pass through the inner court to reach the Holy of Holies. It has to go from our head to our heart before it can enter the spirit. Today, as I was teaching the children how faith steers the Disciple Ship and how to secure each sail, one of the children asked me to explain the basic functions, in order, that a sailor needs to know to operate the ship successfully. I had to think for a few minutes since prayer is as natural as breathing to me, but the Spirit lead me to the answer. I found the order so rewarding, I may work on refining it to teach with. It is real, simple, 'Know what you want or where you want to go.' That is what a prayer is and is the first step toward glory. Then, 'Believe you are going to get there.' You taught us, "When you pray, believe you receive and you shall have whatsoever you say." I have said many times, If you have a care, you have a prayer but you have to believe in order to receive. This is the second step toward glory. Third is to, Pray it through. That is where I spend the most of my time

227

teaching. First a prayer must get into your head, the logic center. There we picture the prayer in shades of gray. Then, as we remain focused on it, it will soon enter our emotional center, out heart and we begin to feel what it would be like when we receive it. But you can't stop there, to pray it through you must see it so vividly that you feel as if you have already got it. A mental picture so vivid that every time you think about it, you instantly feel the joy of having it. One of the girls tells her unbelieving friends, "Seeing is believing but you must believe, in order to see." I tell them that this step brings glory into their heart, even before it shines outward to the world. Then, if they want to be an excellent sailor, they would have to model Daniel. It is said that Daniel had an excellent spirit and he prayed three times daily. I teach them to focus on each prayer, until they feel the glory of it, three times each day and this will move their ship closer to its destination. A sailor would look at each sail several times a day to tighten the ropes or adjust for the wind so they should look at each sail until they feel the holy wind of glory fill their hearts with joy. Then the fifth step is to, take action. Every day to take some action toward each destination or prayer. One of the children was challenged by this and asked, "I thought all I had to do was believe to receive. Isn't it receiving by works if I do it or at least a sign of my unbelief that God will do it?" I smiled and reminded her what James taught us before he came to be with you. "Faith without works is dead. Just like a body without a spirit." I told her that belief was a function of faith, not the other way around. If she was praying for a husband, wouldn't she start making her dress if she really believed? She received the light joyfully and the other students understood that the first sign of unbelief was not taking steps toward your goal. One student said that not taking a step toward each goal daily, belittled a prayer to a wish. Finally, I told them, the sixth step, because God rested on the seventh, was Praise. By the time you have exercised your faith in the five steps, you will have arrived at your destination and that any prayer God has answered is magnified by praise. Tell of his marvelous works, proclaim the goodness of our God and let is Glory fill the earth. For the Glory of God is revealed from faith unto faith and the Holy wind of Praise fills the sails of all Disciple Ships. Lord, I hope this is pleasing to you and that you may extend your arm to many generations. Amen." As I thought how these children were taught to pray and how to function through faith, combined with covenant giving to secure basic needs and aging care, I realized how many monarchs would view this as a threat. In my work at the congressional budget office, I could easily see, if this type Kingdom took off, American policy makers would do everything in their power to tax it to death. This was like an old black and white movie. Old world covenant compared to new world governance creating a battle of values. And if there is one thing I understand, it is values. I close the leather but I notice several more entries. I wasn't about to leave the Bible room without reading the last two diaries. I placed Mary's back in place and reached for the next one. It was packed. It was four times larger than any of the others and felt like it weighed fifty pounds.

Salome's Diary

Suddenly I could smell night air and felt the moisture of a heavy dew. It was unmistakable because it was the identical smell and feel of my evening meetings with Grandpa. Grandma's note said, "Salome was the mother of two disciples, James the Great and John the Revelator. Peter, James and John were the disciples that Jesus took to the mount of transfiguration with him. Salome was also the cousin of Mother Mary and was already a prophetess prior to the upper room baptism. Child, this is Wisdom." I looked at the leather, it was Grandpa's Angel Garden! Etched on the front of the leather was a detailed circular calendar complete with each angel and lines connecting several points. The lines created a geometrical drawing of a pyramid and written beneath the etching was, "I AM the Capstone". There was a different type light coming from the papyrus scrolls. It sparkled like tiny fireflies and swirled around the room and back to the scrolls. Even though the light was so bright it filled the room, I could clearly tell it was like millions upon millions of tiny stars, dancing like galaxies in a night sky. As I opened to the first papyrus it appeared like a open door. It's hard to explain but the words rose up like an opening bloom of a flower until they became legible. I began to read, "And they that shall be of thee shall raise up the foundations of many generations and shall be called the repaired of the breach and the restorer of paths to dwell in." Then, just as the words had risen so I could read them, they drifted backwards until they were gone. I waited to see if something else was going to surface but it didn't. I noticed the tiny stars, as they returned to the diary, seem to be going to the second papyrus scroll so I turned the first one over to reveal the second. This time there appeared to be a sunrise over gorgeous farm land. As I looked upon the papyrus as one would a TV screen, the sun rose until it was blinding to look at. I started to cover my eyes and I noticed words drifting upward blocking out part of the sun's light. They read, "I am the Lord. I change not. I am the same yesterday, today and forever. To every thing there is a season, and a time to every purpose under the heaven. Let there be lights in the firmament of the heaven to divide the day from the night; and let them be for signs, and for seasons, and for days, and years. In your day they shall call unto me, ' We see not our signs: there is no more any prophet: neither is there among us any that knoweth how long. O God, how long shall the adversary reproach?' Where there is no oracle, the people perish. Wherefore, behold, I send unto you prophets, and wise men, and scribes. " Then, just as before, the words drifted back down and the sunlight gave its glory to the moon and on the papyrus was a circular calendar. The tiny stars had all became very still and I sensed I should turn to the next scroll. Not knowing what to expect, I was met with Salome's first entry. "Lord, your mother and I are reaching many years and soon we will be with you. The sisters have asked us to leave our seed for the generation you spoke of being at the end of this age. After meditating about the time you condemned the Pharisee when you said, ' You hypocrites, you can discern the face of the sky and of the earth; but how is it that you do not discern the signs of the time?' I set my heart and mind to study the future as you taught us. I remembered when I taught James and John how to tell time, days, months, yearly seasons and life cycles. I remembered teaching them about the four royal stars of the four horses. I remembered teaching them, as they grew, how each generation had a season, each had life cycles and that the combination of fourteen generations completed one cycle of the seven needed for the Horsemen to return to their original place. I remembered teaching them to number their days so they could apply their hearts toward wisdom, seeing where they were on the map of time and properly navigate in the sea of history. I spoke to cousin Mary earlier today and told her of what I had found, needless to say, your mother was very concerned. John is still evangelizing on the isle of Patmos but your mother and I miss him very much. Please send him home as soon as you can. As I came upon the time you spoke of, I was greatly disturbed as I can only imagine a people going through such a dark time without your covenant. As I lay down for the evening, Lord, I pray that you will give me the words that will speak to the woman you chose in that time. Amen." I turned quickly to the next scroll and began reading. "To my Covenant Sister, Our Lord has chosen you to seed your generation unto salvation. Inorder for you to do this you will have great need to hold hands with Wisdom and see your place in time. Yours is a delicate time and great difficulties exist in my ability to speak to you, in that your generation is now eighty-four years separated from the discipline of wisdom. What I will be able to do is give you many sign posts of changes and beginnings. Specific events I will add in papyruses to come but for now I will begin with the 14th generation in your country, who was born from March 2008. Fourteen generation cycle has great importance in wisdom. In all the generations from Abraham to David are fourteen generations; and from David until the carrying away into Babylon are fourteen generations; and from the carrying away into Babylon unto Christ are fourteen generations. The fourteenth generation always leads the fall of their society and people. Not that they are at fault but victims who are left to see the destruction of a culture ran without wisdom. History reveals every fourth generation has negative or internal reactions to situations beyond their control and having less than good results. Then by November of the year 2015, toward the end of the month, the downward fall into darkness begins and the eternal plowman harnesses his ox as serious change begins toward changing the foundation, roots and heritage of your country. By October 2016 the darkness that began in secret on October 6th, 2012, has begun to become fully visible to the spirit body. In May of 2018 major changes begin and many children are lost. From January 29th, 2016 through October 17th, 2017, capitol is loss and will be unrecoverable by this generation. By February 2019 death arrives to the money changers and the ruler of chaos has begun to deal the cards. By January of 2020 Death has arrived, hand in hand, with the harvester and by March 31st fire rages. By February 2023 the restructuring has took place and the restructuring of family and covenant begins. This is the place you can have the greatest impact in the hourglass of time. This window will remain open until March 2026 and if you are going to have a lasting impact on holding to the foundation and fabric of a covenant nation, this will be your last hope. At the same time in March 2026, A new movement will begin dealing with the foundation and heritage of your country. It will move forward until July and struggle until February 2027 and then begin to settle in and move forward. Be a part of that change because by July of 2028 this change becomes a visible part of your country. The Recovery Generation begins to be born, by January 2024. Spend much, much, much time with these children, they will affect outcomes and society for well over a hundred years. You will be aging in grace if you care much for these children. Teach them Faith. Be their Faith Coach all the way to your grave. Invest your life into them, they hold the keys to the Kingdom! By the time they reach 2043, the next generation is beginning to be born. Theirs will be cautiously quiet, who's impact will be modest in light of their parents. By March of 2039 power and pride has returned to family and vision has returned to save the children. If only I had time to carry you year by year or even greater, month by month, but my heart is heavy for you because you must go through so much to reach the children at the exact moment in time. I must end for now but I will begin listing major events, both good and bad, so you can prepare your disciples for them, in the papyruses to come. May God Bless, Salome." I sat there digesting every word. I thought how I had always considered people in distant history as, somewhat, uneducated or at least unlearned. Salome was far from stupid. Apparently, her grip on the circular calendar was elite and seeing how she was the mother of two disciples made discounting her words, all the more difficult. In my jobs at both the Census Bureau and the Congressional Budget Office, I had ran population models well into the twenty second century based on resource management but I had never imagined running social science and cognitive science models alongside game theory war and disaster models. As I place Salome's diary to the sided, I realized that man is just a speck on the time line of history and if I was going to have any spot in history, I had better start mapping out the trajectory. I reach into the chest and pulled out the last diary.

Mother Mary's Diary

As I touched the diary, it was noticeably soft, like a super soft pillow. I carefully looked at the etchings on the leather. At first, I thought it was a bleeding heart but as I looked closer it was a crying heart. The heart was etched in such a way that it appeared to be crying tears and the tear drops fell to the ground and form the words, 'The Children'. I opened to the first papyrus scroll and began reading, "Some give their money. Some give their time. But Abraham gave his child. And so, I gave mine." I realized I was holding the diary of the mother of Jesus! I began to tremble and closed the leather and held it against my chest. I saw, in my spirit, her hands picking up her son from the manger. I saw her covering him with blankets on cold winter nights and kissing him on the forehead and saying good night. I saw her watching him preach from a mountain side and I saw her holding him for the last time before he made his way to Jerusalem. Then I saw tears rolling down her cheeks just as I realized mine were now. I opened my leather heart, determined to absorb every drop. She began, "Please forgive my trembling hands and the tear drop ink stained papyrus but my spirit has seen the people of your day and I cannot hold back my sorrow for them. I am so very sorry they have never known the Love of a covenant family. I am so very sorry they have never known true Love. I feel sorrow for them that have never know real trust. I feel sorrow for the abandoned child. I feel sorrow for the divorced. Great sorrow I feel because they have never known covenant or felt the solid rock foundation of true Love. Great sorrow fills my heart at the thought of a whole generation never understanding what our covenant is. Never knowing the peace or the security or the stability of a covenant store house or a covenant friend who is really, there in their time of need. My heart has great sorrow for yours is a generation that uses people to get things and ours uses things to join people. Great sorrow I feel for the children who never had a chance and because of this, judgment must come. Our God cannot and will not lie and he said that every man's work will be tested by fire and your generations will not be exempt. God cut covenant with Abraham to reach the children and your governments have chosen commerce over conscience. Keep the Sabbath Holy was not for God's benefit, it is for yours. When a people will not keep one day to teach their children's conscience, a society has chosen commerce as their God and soon the river dries up, enemies invade the land and evil spirits are released and abound. Each time blood flows, each time the cries get louder and louder and each time I weep. I do not weep for those that have chosen their way. I do not weep for those that die. I do not weep for those that suffer. I weep for my God's heart was extended to you and by commerce you placed little value on it. His loving arms reached for you, longing for you to enter in to the covenant but your self will would not release you. You could not die to self-worship. And as my son wept for Jerusalem, I weep for you, because my heart is sorry for all the joys we have and you have not yet even experienced." There were several blurred words where tear stains made it difficult to read but I just sat there and stared. I was reading a letter that was writing to me, just for me, by the mother of the Son of God. I couldn't get my mind wrapped around it. This was an experience outside anything imaginable and yet, I had a sense that my tornado was about to explode. I turned to the next papyrus and continued, "After much prayer and meditation, our Father has given me to you. You are now, my child, and as I taught my son, so shall I teach you. You are not the Lamb of God as he was but you are a High Priestess of the Covenant and you will be given dominion over a jurisdiction. You will be given many disciples and your duty is to present them to God, without spot or blemish. In order, for you to accomplish this you must embody the duties of the old priest. The priest would encounter a troubled soul and would view them as a cup filled with all the information they had learned, things they had heard, seen and or experienced. The priest saw his duty to clean the cup then to present a clean cup to the Lord, thus creating a cup worthy to enter the covenant. My Son gave you authority to bind anything unclean or unhealthy and cast it out of their cup. He then gave you authority to lose, into the cup, the joy, peace, security, love or whatever spirit you found necessary for strength. You are a High Priestess, you have authority, use it! I do not have time to cover spirits but let me illustrate your authority. You see a child fallen, down in the street, as you come closer to assist, you see several chariots approaching. You rush into the street and raise your hand for them to stop and they do. You motion one to go to the right, and it does. You motion to the other to go left and it does. Why? Are you bigger than the chariots? Are you stronger? No, they recognize you have taken authority and obey by the law of spirit. Authority is something you must exercise, it is not jewelry. If you exercise it, the earth will be filled with his glory and your faith will be fruitful and multiply. The earth is your garden, fill it with your children of faith. Fill their cups with faith and our covenant will overtake the darkness that is coming in your day. The darkness is real, it is not stoppable because God has ordained the judgment of the wicked and unbelievers but if you take heed, you will overcome and shine. When our covenant was taken from Egypt, they experienced ten plagues. We did not so our God could show the world his glory. You do not have to experience the judgments but you do have to be in a covenant like ours. A real covenant, not those imitations of your time. There was a time when your country was young, when a father who had land would grow extra food for those that might need. There was a time that having family was greater than having money. I remember, as a child, walking through a beautiful orchard and my father picking fruit for us to eat and even though we did not know the owner by name, it was a covenant man and his garden was freely ours. I remember a time that we did not need kings or judges. The prophets helped us forecast times of drought and bad events. We listened and were blessed but when we didn't listen repentance was a season. I remember when covenant worked because love was the rule and when covenant didn't work, it was because caring and giving were the exception. Covenant works when the people have purpose and principles combined with a prophet that can create clarity for proper navigation and direction. Covenant is destroyed when its members begin seeking power and pleasure and the prophet cast blindness by withholding the vision. You are my High Priestess child. I will not leave you sightless so commit to study the spirit of names. It is a great secret and it will never fail to show you the spirit within the cup. Whatsoever Adam named them, that was the spirit nature of it. If a parent names a child after a person they know, the child will unknowingly perform the dance of that spirit until you free them. It is the duty of the priest. If you change the name, you change the spirit. You must help them become someone in order, for them to accomplish something. You are now High Priestess Faith Coach, child of Mary. A High Priestess who ministers Faith, who knows the way and will carry many through the greatest darkness since the world began. Teach faith, baptize and start covenants from town to town, it is your only hope and when you have finished, Heaven awaits. Heaven is a covenant people. A true and unashamed love that has overcame all challenges to is love and grows greater and greater with every new member. Heaven is where all love abides. Every thought anyone has ever thought about true love is here. All, of your loved ones who had love in their heart is here. Every imagination of what true love could be is here. And every thought or memory you ever have about love is your personal glimpse of Heaven's gates. I and my covenant with you are here. Enter by the South Gate and you will find me waiting for you by the Tumbling Waters."

Other Books by your Authors

Invisible Keys

Faith Coaching 2018 Prayer Journal

E-4 Option

Macedonian Oracle

New Books coming Soon

I Will

Faith Coaching

Coaching Series and Work Books

I Am

A Child is Given

Spiritology

Tehillah

Righteous Rangers

The Leader I Love

And many more.....

www.ingramcontent.com/pod-product-compliance
Lightning Source LLC
Chambersburg PA
CBHW030537030726
47495CB00004B/1032